She Never Wanted to Visit the Fear Mansion Again. . . .

"Come again soon, Julia!" Angelica called.

That brought Jenna to a stop. Slowly, she turned toward Angelica. She suddenly felt cold, as if someone had replaced her blood with ice water.

"You mean Jenna, don't you, Mrs. Fear?" she asked.

"That's what I said, dear," Angelica replied.

Jenna studied her for a moment. Then she turned and started walking again. Faster this time. She couldn't wait to get away from there. Angelica might have *thought* she'd said "Jenna." But she hadn't. She'd said "Julia."

She'd mistaken her for Julia Fear.

Her dead daughter.

FEAR STREET SAGAS® #6
R·L·STINE

Daughters of Silence

A Parachute Press Book

AN ARCHWAY PAPERBACK
Published by POCKET BOOKS
New York London Toronto Sydney Tokyo Singapore

This book is a work of fiction. Names, characters, places and incidents are products of the author's imagination or are used fictitiously. Any resemblance to actual events or locales or persons, living or dead, is entirely coincidental.

AN ARCHWAY PAPERBACK *Original*

 An Archway Paperback published by
POCKET BOOKS, a division of Simon & Schuster Inc.
1230 Avenue of the Americas, New York, NY 10020

Copyright © 1997 by Parachute Press, Inc.

DAUGHTERS OF SILENCE WRITTEN BY WENDY HALEY

All rights reserved, including the right to reproduce
this book or portions thereof in any form whatsoever.
For information address Pocket Books, 1230 Avenue
of the Americas, New York, NY 10020

ISBN: 0-671-00293-7

First Archway Paperback printing April 1997

10 9 8 7 6 5 4 3 2 1

FEAR STREET is a registered trademark of
Parachute Press, Inc.

AN ARCHWAY PAPERBACK and colophon are
registered trademarks of Simon & Schuster Inc.

Cover art by Lisa Falkenstern

Printed in the U.S.A.

IL 7+

Daughters of Silence

Chapter
1

Shadyside Village
1878

"Shadyside Station! Next stop!" Jenna heard the conductor shout.

She looked up from her book. Had they reached Shadyside already?

As she felt the train slow down, her heartbeat quickened. She couldn't wait to see her best friend Hallie again!

Peering out her window, she saw the village of Shadyside coming into view. Crowded with wagons and horses and buggies, the town's wide Main Street bustled with midday shoppers. Jenna spotted a big general store, a bake shop, and a post office.

Just past Main Street, Jenna caught sight of pretty white houses, standing side by side on quiet, tree-lined lanes.

"Shadyside Village," the conductor called again

1

from the front of the car. "If you're getting off at Shadyside, folks, better get packed up."

Jenna looked outside again and spotted Hallie and her parents on the platform. She leaned out of the window as far as she dared.

"Hallie! Over here!" she called, waving frantically.

"Jenna!" Hallie squealed as she waved back.

Hallie lifted her skirts and ran alongside the slowly moving train. Her curly blond hair lifted on the breeze and her blue eyes sparkled with excitement. Jenna rose from her seat, then grabbed her carpetbag. The fabric of her long dress and petticoat swished as she hurried toward the front of the car.

As the train wheels ground to a stop, she flew down the stairs and straight into Hallie's arms.

Hallie swept her up in a tight hug. "You wouldn't believe how much I missed you!" she exclaimed.

"Well, you're the one who moved away," Jenna teased, pushing her friend out to arm's length. "I declare, you've grown a foot!"

"Before you know it, I'll be as tall as you," Hallie retorted. "Oh, Jenna, I'm so glad you could spend the whole summer with me. We're going to have such fun!"

Jenna smiled and squeezed Hallie's hand. Hallie was her best friend in all the world. As close as sisters, her parents always said. Jenna wished they really *could* be sisters.

"I can see that you two girls aren't wasting any time catching up, are you?" Jenna heard Hallie's father declare with a laugh.

She turned to see Hallie's parents standing right

beside her. Mr. Sheridan still looked tall and thin. His wide smile made her feel warm and welcomed. He wore a dark suit and a high, starched collar. His thick black mustache curled up at the ends, adding to his refined air. Mrs. Sheridan looked as pretty as ever. From beneath the rim of her stylish bonnet, her bright blue eyes sparkled as she greeted Jenna.

"Welcome to our new home, dear," she murmured. "We're so glad to have you!"

"Thank you for inviting me," Jenna replied, remembering her mother's instructions about minding her manners.

"Let me take your bags, Jenna," Mr. Sheridan offered. He picked up a large suitcase that the conductor had carried off the train for her.

"I'll take the carpetbag," Hallie insisted. She grabbed up the smaller bag, then linked her arm with Jenna's as they followed Hallie's parents to the street.

Mr. Sheridan led them to an open carriage where two horses patiently waited, tethered to a post. He set down the suitcase and helped the girls climb in. Jenna took a place next to Hallie on the seat facing forward and Mrs. Sheridan sat on the seat opposite. After tying her case in the back, Mr. Sheridan hopped up on the driver's bench and took the reins.

"Gidd-up," Mr. Sheridan called to the horses. Kicking up a cloud of dust with their lively gait, the horses set off on the road that led away from the station and village. Their hoofbeats made a gentle *clop-clop* sound on the hard-packed road. Jenna relaxed and watched the passing scenery.

Mrs. Sheridan opened her parasol with a snap. "I've made your favorite dessert for tonight, Jenna."

"Peach pie?" Jenna felt her mouth water as she said the words aloud.

Mrs. Sheridan shook her head. *"Two* peach pies."

Jenna spotted a group of young men and women who'd gathered in front of the saddle shop to talk. They seemed right around her and Hallie's age. One girl waved, but the others just watched curiously as the carriage passed by.

"Do you like it here?" Jenna asked, turning back to her friend.

The other girl shrugged. "It's all right, I suppose. But everyone else has lived here forever. It's hard to make friends."

"You will," her mother promised. "It just takes time."

"Well, Jenna's here now," Hallie told her. "And we're going to have fun all summer long."

A short time later, Mr. Sheridan turned the horses down a quiet lane on the eastern edge of town and then onto a gravel drive.

"Look, Jenna. There's our house," Hallie announced brightly.

A short distance down the gravel drive, Jenna spotted a pale yellow two-story house with dark-green shutters and a tall brick chimney. The house sat on a long green lawn and several old oak trees made the place look shady and cool. She liked the wide front porch with its flower boxes and wooden swing.

"How pretty!" she exclaimed.

Mrs. Sheridan smiled at her response.

"Here we are. Watch your step getting out, ladies," Mr. Sheridan announced as he brought the carriage to a halt at the front of the house.

Jenna breathed in the fresh scents of the blooming flowers and clean country air. A tantalizing aroma of food wafted on the breeze and she felt her mouth water. "Hmmm, something smells delicious," she noticed.

"Cook should have supper all ready for us," Mrs. Sheridan returned. "Girls, you go wash up while I help Cook put the dishes out."

Jenna followed Hallie out of the carriage and into the house. It felt like home to her at once. This was going to be a wonderful summer, she thought.

After a delicious meal, including two slices of peach pie each, she and Hallie sat out on the porch swing. It was fully dark now, and the shadowy places beneath the oak trees looked velvety thick and soft. Jenna watched a sliver of moon rise slowly in the sky. She felt a soft breeze whisper past her cheek and heard the tree branches creak and sigh.

Jenna pulled her feet up onto the seat and wrapped her arms around her knees.

"Remember how we used to stay up late and tell ghost stories?" Hallie asked suddenly.

"Do I ever," Jenna replied. She poked Hallie in the shoulder. "Remember when you told me that story about the Green Man? I guess we were only about eight or nine years old."

"You thought it was true," Hallie added, grinning.

"I didn't sleep for a month," Jenna told her. "I kept

waiting to hear him scratching on my window with his long, jagged fingernails. I could have strangled you when I found out you'd made up the whole thing."

"I bet I could still make your hair stand on end, Jen," Hallie teased.

"Not anymore," Jenna retorted. "I'm too old to fall for your wild stories, Hallie."

"Sure you are," Hallie agreed with a teasing grin. "So you won't mind strolling over to the graveyard tonight? I've got a great story to tell you that I heard around town and it would be way more fun to tell it in just the right setting."

Jenna's spine tingled with unease. "A graveyard?"

"You're not scared, are you?" Hallie challenged.

"Of course not!" Jenna retorted. "There's nothing to be afraid of in a graveyard."

Then she realized that Hallie had done it again. Well, actually, Jenna realized, she'd trapped herself. She shot Hallie a simmering glare. But Hallie only smiled at her.

Finally, Jenna smiled back. "You're a twit, Hallie. All right, I'll go. But it's your fault if we have nightmares for the next ten years."

"Come on," Hallie called eagerly. "Follow me." She ran off the porch and across the front lawn. Jenna caught up with her out on the street.

They walked quickly and passed two other houses where Jenna saw the front parlor windows glowing with warm light. She felt a sudden urge to turn back. Then she bit down on her lip and kept walking.

The street grew darker as only moonlight lit their way. Jenna noticed that the houses had disappeared. On either side of the road she saw only a stretch of thick woods. The damp leaves and twisting tree trunks glimmered in the moon's silvery light.

"Maybe we should have brought along a lamp," Jenna suggested.

"Too late now," Hallie replied with a shrug. "Look, there's the entrance."

Up ahead, Jenna suddenly spotted two tall marble pillars covered with patches of green moss. A wrought-iron arch stretched between the pillars. She could barely make out the curling letters of the sign on the arch. She paused and squinted up at it.

"Shadyside Cemetery," she slowly read aloud.

"What did you think it would say?" Hallie chided. "Come on, slowpoke," Hallie urged as she grabbed Jenna's arm. "We don't have all night. My parents will wonder what happened to us."

Jenna felt her friend tug her through the gate. The sign's shadow fell across Jenna's face as she passed beneath it, and she felt her body tremble with an involuntary shudder.

"This is a creepy place," she whispered.

"Why are you whispering?" Hallie asked. "It's not like anyone can hear us."

"I . . ." With a laugh, Jenna threw up her hands. "You're right. I suppose I whispered because . . . everyone whispers in graveyards, don't they?"

"I guess they do," Hallie agreed, leading the way deeper into the cemetery's dark shadows. Rocky and choked with weeds, the winding path curled around the rows of headstones. Jenna felt hard stones press through the soft soles of her shoes. In the pale moonlight the rows of headstones looked like jagged teeth poking up from the earth.

A thick mist clung to the ground and the breeze sent pale gray tendrils coiling along the path and around the stone slabs. The air smelled wet. And with each breath Jenna noticed a taint of something else, a repulsive, foul scent she couldn't quite recognize.

"Look!" Hallie cried, pointing at a large, dark shape ahead.

Jenna squinted into the shadows. After a moment, her eyes adjusted and she could make out a small, square building with a domed roof. As they walked closer, Jenna saw a figure perched over the entryway, just in front of the dome.

They stood in front of the marble building and Jenna looked up at the figure. A statue of an angel, she realized. Nothing that unusual to find in a cemetery. Many people liked the idea of placing such a stone guardian over the resting place of a loved one.

But this had to be the most hideous angel she'd ever seen. The most menacing, malevolent guardian.

Carved in black marble and covered with patches of slimy green moss, its monstrous face wore a snarling, sinister expression. Jenna felt a shiver race down her spine as she gazed up at its disturbing face. The sightless eyes bulged out of their sockets and its thick lips curled ominously, baring long, pointed teeth.

Green moss, like spiderwebs, hung from the heavy black wings. Wings that to Jenna looked far too large for the angel's emaciated body. Hunched around bony, slouched shoulders, the long feathers tapered to knife-edge points. Jenna's gaze rested on the angel's hands: gnarled claws, folded and clasped to its sunken chest.

"What is this place?" Jenna stammered.

"It's a mausoleum," Hallie whispered. "The Fear girls are buried in there. People say their ghosts roam this place."

Jenna swallowed hard. "There's no such thing as ghosts, Hallie," she declared.

Hallie leaned her back against a nearby headstone. "Maybe once you hear this story, you'll change your mind about that."

Jenna crossed her arms over her chest. "I doubt it."

"Okay, we'll see." Hallie tossed her head back and slowly smiled. "Here's the story. There are awful rumors about the Fears here in Shadyside. Terrible stories . . . They say that Simon and Angelica Fear are evil. They say that their daughters died violently. One of the sisters killed the other. And because the girls died violently, their spirits are tied to this place forever."

The wind tossed the branches of the trees, filling the night with whispers. Jenna could almost imagine voices amid the rustling. She could almost imagine someone watching her from the shadows. She resisted the urge to glance over her shoulder. Or up at the hideous angel.

"But that's not even the worst," Hallie told her. "People say . . ." She paused for dramatic effect. Her words sounded in a husky whisper. "They say that when the Fear girls were buried, their bodies had no bones! They say there are nights when the girls' skeletons walk, not dead, yet not at rest. Forever searching for a way to come back to life."

Jenna's eerie mood vanished. "Hallie, that is really too much. I'd believe in ghosts before I'd believe that *ridiculous* story."

"Well, maybe you wouldn't say that if you ever saw the look on people's faces around here whenever the name Fear is mentioned."

"What kind of look?" Jenna asked.

"Well, almost as if they're . . . terrified."

Jenna sighed. "Hallie, you're too gullible. Remember, you're new in town. Whoever told you that wild story was only teasing you. They probably laughed all the way home."

"Oh, Jenna! Sometimes I think you're way too sensible for your own good," Hallie remarked.

"Oh, Jenna, yourself," she retorted. "Look, we'll prove it. We'll walk right up to that mausoleum, and you'll see for yourself that there are no ghouls or ghosts or dancing skeletons anywhere around here."

Hallie's eyes glinted as she looked around. "Are you sure that's a good idea?"

"Anything that will make you stop believing that wild story is a good idea. Now come on." Taking Hallie by the hand, Jenna started walking toward the crypt.

Dry leaves rustled underfoot as they made their way through the gravestones. Jenna glanced up at the angel statue. It loomed above them, looking even larger and more menacing.

"Can you see the inscription yet?" Hallie asked.

Jenna squinted at the letters carved above the lintel. For a moment, they seemed almost to squirm. "All I can make out from here are the names and dates. Julia Fear and Hannah Fear. They were almost the same ages as we are when they died. How sad."

A cloud passed over the moon, plunging the cemetery into total darkness. Jenna looked up. Everything looked and felt different. The headstones seemed to shift into twisted, shadowy shapes. Coils of mist looped up from the ground, alive and seeking . . . something. All around, the trees muttered and groaned with a hundred voices.

Then the air turned cold. Impossibly cold. Enfolding her like an icy shroud, numbing her body until only fear remained. Unable to take another step, she stopped.

As suddenly as it had come, the cold vanished. Jenna shook her head. It had all happened so fast . . . It couldn't have been real. Her imagination had been playing tricks on her, no doubt.

And then the clouds passed, revealing the moon once more. Jenna stared down at the inscription again.

"Hallie!" she called, her heart beating hard, pounding its way right out of her chest.

The other girl turned. "Jenna, what's the matter?"

"The inscription!" Jenna hissed, forcing the words up through a throat gone tight with fear. "It says, 'Hannah and Julia, beloved daughters of Simon and Angelica Fear.' And it says . . . It says . . ."

"What?" Hallie demanded impatiently.

Jenna took a deep breath. "It says, *'They are not dead.'*"

Chapter
2

"What did you say?" Hallie's eyes opened wide. The whites of her eyes gleamed in the dimness.

"Look for yourself," Jenna urged. "It's right there!"

" 'They are not dead,' " Hallie read.

The girls stood staring at each other for a moment. Jenna wanted to say something sensible, but her throat felt dry and choked with fear.

A deep, eerie sound broke the silence. It sounded to Jenna like someone moaning. The mournful noise seemed to echo from all directions at once. Hallie gasped. She clutched Jenna's arm so hard it hurt.

"W-what was that?" Hallie whispered.

"An owl," Jenna whispered back. "I think."

Hallie tugged at her arm. "Let's get out of here."

The breeze wafted through the trees. Branches tossed back and forth. Dark shadows leaped across the front of the mausoleum. Jenna leaned forward as she saw something dark spattered across the lower part of the inscription.

Jenna let her breath out in a huge sigh. "Look, Hallie. Some mud or dirt is hiding some of the words."

"I don't want to know any more," Hallie hissed.

"Nonsense. There's always a sensible explanation for these things," Jenna insisted. "Just wait one more minute."

Jenna reached out to touch the inscription. The dark substance crumbled beneath her fingertips, leaving grit on her skin.

"Don't touch it!" Hallie cried.

"Hallie, it's only dirt," Jenna told her.

"Oh." Hallie heaved a sigh. "I thought it was blood or something."

Jenna smiled at her friend. "You really are a twit. Now, let's see what this really says."

She scraped at the crusted dirt with her thumbnail. It flaked away easily, leaving the inscription bare.

" 'They are not dead,' " she read, running her finger along the carved letters. " 'They live eternally in our hearts.' "

Hallie giggled. That started Jenna laughing, too, and soon they were gasping for breath.

"Can you believe we were such chickens?" Hallie asked.

Jenna had to take several breaths before she could answer. "They are not dead," she repeated in a hollow, spooky tone.

Hallie burst into another fit of giggling. Jenna started laughing again, too. She laughed so hard, she felt her sides ache and tears well up in the corner of her eyes.

"Oh, that was good," Hallie gasped. "You should have seen the look on your face, Jenna."

"The look on my face?" Jenna gasped. "You looked pale as a—"

"Don't say it!" Hallie gasped. "If I start laughing again, I don't think I'll be able to stop."

"Me, either."

Jenna looked up at the angel. She suddenly felt her mirth drain away, replaced by a frigid chill. The statue's gaze seemed fixed upon her, its clawlike hands ready to stretch out and snatch her up.

Jenna took a stumbling step backward, away from the mausoleum. Time to go, she thought. She looked over at Hallie. Her friend stood in front of the door. Her hand rested on the ornate wrought-iron door latch.

"Hey, it's unlocked," Hallie exclaimed, her voice quivering with excitement. "Let's go in!"

Jenna wiped her damp hands on her gown. Sudden dread gripped her stomach with cold, clammy fingers. "In . . . there?"

"Why not?"

"It's a grave, Hallie."

"All the better." Hallie shot her a look. "Unless you want to admit there's a reason to be afraid?"

Jenna lifted her chin defiantly. "Of course not!"

"Then let's go."

Hallie turned the latch and gave the door a push. It swung open soundlessly. Jenna blinked in surprise. She'd expected the hinges to squeak from disuse. Strange.

She peered over Hallie's shoulder. Dark shadows filled the crypt, shifting and swirling like thick, black smoke. Jenna coughed as she breathed in the musty, damp air. It smelled stale. Unpleasant. Her stomach lurched uneasily as she caught another scent, a sickly sweet, rotten odor.

Jenna's heart pounded double-time. She did not want to go in there.

"Here's a candle," Hallie said, reaching up to a tiny shelf just outside the door. "And I've got matches right here in my pocket."

Hallie struck the match on the marble door frame, and Jenna blinked against the flare of light. Holding the candle, Hallie stepped into the mausoleum.

Jenna wasn't about to let her friend go in alone. Still, her feet felt suddenly glued to her place outside. *Don't be silly,* she told herself firmly.

"Hallie?" she called. Her friend did not answer. Jenna peered into the shadows and spotted the flickering light of Hallie's small candle.

The breeze swirled against her back. The smell of decay grew stronger. She coughed and covered her mouth with her hand.

An odd feeling tugged at her awareness. She felt as if someone were calling to her. But not with words. She had a sudden urge to look up.

She didn't want to. But that odd feeling nagged at her, tipping her head back before she could stop herself.

Jenna gazed up.

Her breath went in, but it didn't go out again. Instead, it stayed there, hot and hurting, while her heart tried to beat its way right out of her chest.

The angel was watching her.

Its eyes had no irises, no pupils. But it saw her. Jenna could feel its menacing stare.

For a moment, she thought she heard the sound of ruffling feathers, then saw those marble wings quiver ever so slightly.

About to take flight.

About to swoop down and snatch her up.

With a gasp, she turned to run.

"Jenna!" Hallie cried as she rushed out of the mausoleum.

Jenna ignored her. All she wanted to do was run and run and run and never come back. But Hallie soon caught up with her, grabbed her by the arm, and dragged her to a stop.

"What's wrong with you?" Hallie demanded. "What happened?"

Too frightened to speak, Jenna pointed at the angel. To her astonishment, its eyes were closed.

Hallie frowned. "What about the angel?"

"It . . . looked at me."

"That's impossible," Hallie said.

"It looked at me," Jenna insisted. "Its eyes were open and it looked at me!"

Hallie stared at her as if she'd lost her mind. "Jenna, it's a statue. It can't open its eyes."

Jenna shook her head. She couldn't believe this. It had seemed so real, so terribly real. "I . . . suppose not," she muttered. "But I was so sure."

"You're letting your imagination run away with you," Hallie told her. Sudden mischief sparkled in her eyes. "Now this is a first. Sensible Jenna, getting so spooked that you thought a marble angel opened its eyes and looked at you."

"Its eyes were open before. I swear it," Jenna insisted. "Big, bulging eyes," she added with a sudden shiver. "Didn't you notice before?"

"No, I guess I didn't," Hallie replied. "And I guess I didn't notice that it was ready to fly down from its perch . . . and *get you!*" Hallie cried, swooping at Jenna with her arms outstretched like wings.

Jenna laughed and fended Hallie off. She felt glad that the other girl's silliness had chased away her heart-stopping terror.

"Come on, let's see the inside of the mausoleum, and then we'll go," Hallie suggested. "Then, when people in town start their wild Fear stories, we can tell them how we walked straight into that crypt and came out again."

Jenna tried to ignore the shudder that raced up her spine. She'd let her imagination run away with her once. She wasn't going to let it happen again. Gritting her teeth, she forced herself to look up at the angel. Its eyes remained closed. It didn't look back at her.

Of course. It was a statue, after all. Only a statue.

She took a deep breath and followed Hallie into the crypt, feeling only the faintest twitch of dread as she walked under the angel.

Hallie's candle sent yellow light dancing around the room. The walls, floor, and even the single bench in the center were carved from black marble. The soft sound of their breathing bounced back at them from the stone.

"Where are they?" Hallie whispered, stopping just inside the door.

Jenna could see that two bronze squares had been set in the far wall of the crypt to mark the resting place of the Fear girls. Dampness had turned the metal blue-green.

"Those plaques say something," she replied as curiosity overtook her misgivings.

She took the candle from Hallie and raised it high as she walked closer to the plaques. The smell of decayed flowers grew stronger. Finally, she could see the lettering.

Julia Fear. Hannah Fear. The names had been etched deeply into the bronze, as though someone had wanted to make sure they'd never disappear. Poor girls, Jenna thought. They'd been so young. That terrible story about them couldn't be true.

"I wonder what really happened to you," she murmured. "Poor Hannah. Poor Julia."

Some impulse made her lay her palm on the plaque marking Julia's grave. She hadn't planned to do that. But the urge had been too strong to ignore, and she'd moved before she realized what she was doing.

The metal felt warm. Warm as . . . her own skin. Strange, when the rest of the crypt felt so chilly and damp.

Startled by a faint rustling sound behind her, Jenna whirled around.

A tall, thin figure filled the doorway. Dressed all in white. Shadows hid its face. As it took a slow, single step forward, the breeze billowed in the fabric of its long, flowing gown.

Jenna's legs went numb.

Unaware, Hallie stood unmoving. Behind her, the apparition seemed to float on the wind.

"Hallie!" Jenna whispered.

"What is it now?" the other girl impatiently replied.

Jenna opened her mouth to speak. But all that came out was a strangled, choking sound. She raised her trembling hand and pointed.

"Behind you!" she croaked.

Hallie stared at her for a moment, then turned. Jenna saw the candle drop from her hand. The light sputtered out, plunging the vault into total darkness.

Jenna heard her friend's deep, rasping gasp.

Then an earsplitting scream.

Chapter
3

"How ow dare you!" the apparition growled in the pitch-black gloom.

Silhouetted by the moonlight, Jenna watched breathlessly as the apparition slowly raised long, bony arms, its clawlike hands stretching out from the shadows to grab her.

Jenna squeezed her eyes shut and clung to Hallie's trembling body. *The angel,* she thought. *I desecrated the graves it protected, and now it's come for me.*

"Look at me!" the apparition demanded. Jenna slowly opened her eyes. In the silvery moonglow, Jenna could see the phantom pointing directly at her. A wild gust of wind swept into the crypt and the apparition's long, unbound hair swirled around its head.

She stared at the long, skeletal finger, expecting lightning to stab out and burn her to ash. Hallie clung to her and whimpered. She pressed her face against Jenna's arm.

"What are you doing in here?" the apparition demanded.

Jenna picked up her head and tried to speak. But each time she looked directly at the looming figure, her body convulsed with a violent chill. She fought against the sensation. Tried to shake it off. No use.

Jenna glanced up at the mysterious figure and her teeth chattered in her mouth. Bone-penetrating cold pierced her body with a thousand icy needles. She hugged herself and dropped to the floor, crouched in a cramped, shivering ball. Beside her, Hallie looked as if she felt the same.

"I asked you a question!" the raspy voice shrieked, echoing off the stone walls. "Wicked, wicked girls!"

"W-we just wanted to see—" Jenna managed to mumble.

"How dare you!" the ghostly figure screamed. "How dare you disturb my daughters' resting place!"

My *daughters?* This was no apparition. No sinister, avenging angel, Jenna realized.

Only one person could be standing in the doorway.

Angelica Fear.

Jenna dared to peer at Angelica Fear. She quickly scuttled to her feet. Then reached down and pulled Hallie up.

Oh, no! They were in big trouble now. Jenna glanced at Hallie. But the other girl just stood with her hand over her mouth and her eyes round with fear. Obviously, Jenna would have to handle any explanations.

"Ma'am," she whispered. "Mrs. Fear—"

"Light your candle," the woman ordered. "I want to see your faces. Vile little vandals. I want to look into the eyes of girls who would desecrate the graves of my darling daughters."

Jenna bent and grabbed the candle off the floor. Quickly, Hallie scrabbled in her pocket for a match, then relit the flame. Jenna's hand shook just a little as she turned toward Mrs. Fear. But the woman's face remained in shadow.

"We didn't mean any disrespect, ma'am," Jenna assured her. "We didn't damage anything. We were only curious."

"Curious?" Angelica asked. "About what?"

Jenna felt her cheeks grow hot with embarrassment. "We, ah, heard some stories—"

"Ah, yes," Angelica groaned. "I've heard the awful things they say about my daughters. My poor girls," she sniffed. "Nobody knows how they suffered." She sighed. "Still suffer," she whispered, covering her eyes with a thin, pale hand.

Silence settled over the crypt. Jenna didn't dare speak. She could hear only Angelica Fear's sighs and Hallie's quick shallow breaths.

Suddenly, Angelica Fear dropped her hand and pinned Jenna with a penetrating stare. "And who in the world are you?" she demanded in an icy tone.

"I'm Jenna Hanson. This is my friend, Hallie Sheridan." Taking a deep breath, she went on. "Hallie's family just moved to Shadyside, and I came to spend the summer with them. We're best friends. Actually, we're as close as sisters—"

Angelica stepped into the crypt, and Jenna finally got a good look at her. Her black hair shimmered with the iridescent sheen of a raven's feathers. A thick lock of white hair, startling in contrast, caught the candle-light in a silver gleam. Her cheekbones were high and sharp, her cheeks hollow. Below swooping black brows, hard, green eyes glittered like emeralds.

Jenna thought she was very beautiful. But some-thing about her looks struck Jenna as peculiar. Unset-tling.

"Sisters," Angelica mused. "Yes."

Jenna waited for her to say something else. But she didn't. The silence stretched uncomfortably.

"There's no good excuse for us trespassing, Mrs. Fear," Jenna said. "All we can do is apologize. And promise never to do it again."

Angelica's eyelids drifted closed for a moment. Then she opened them, her gaze boring straight into Jenna. Jenna told herself they were ordinary eyes, belonging to an ordinary woman. But here in her daughters' crypt, Angelica's eyes looked like clear, hard glass. And as violent and cruel as a green-tinged tornado sky.

Then she blinked, and the violence and cruelty vanished. As though it had never been. Jenna won-dered if she'd even seen it at all.

"Your apology is accepted," Angelica quietly re-plied. "But now that I've found you here, you must stay and talk for a while. You must tell me a little more about yourselves, Jenna and Hallie."

"I'm sorry, Mrs. Fear, but I don't think we can—" Hallie spluttered.

"Of course you can. You must!" At Angelica's sharp interruption every muscle in Jenna's body tensed into a hard knot. Jenna barely drew a breath as she watched Angelica push a strand of jet-black hair off her face. Heavy jewels on her thin fingers flashed in the candlelight.

"You see, I come here whenever I feel lonely," Angelica softly murmured. "It comforts me to visit with my daughters . . ."

"Ma'am—" Jenna began.

"These stories they tell about my girls . . ." Angelica continued as though Jenna hadn't spoken at all. "They're not true, girls. You must not believe them," she insisted with a sharp shake of her head. "Once the rumors got started, there was nothing we could do to stop them. Perhaps it's the name. 'Fear' tends to create a certain response in people. It's only natural, I suppose . . ." Her raspy voice trailed off.

She gazed at the far wall, looking lost in thought. Jenna wondered if she had forgotten them. Maybe they could sneak out. She glanced at Hallie over her shoulder. *Let's get out of here!* she mouthed silently.

Hallie nodded. They started edging toward the door.

Then Angelica pinned them with a hard stare. All the vagueness in her eyes vanished like smoke. Meeting that gaze was like being pierced with a sharp stick. Jenna felt frozen in her tracks.

Still watching them, Angelica Fear strolled to the plaque marking Hannah's grave. Her fingers looked so pale to Jenna that they almost seemed translucent as she laid them on the bronze.

"They said such terrible things about my girls," she murmured. "How could anyone think that one of my girls could have killed the other? My girls loved each other. I tried not to listen to those monstrous stories. I tried not to care."

Angelica dropped her hand to her side. The wind swirled into the crypt. The candle flame danced and flickered. For a moment, Angelica Fear's eyes looked as deep and black as the night sky. Jenna's skin crawled with a sudden, powerful dread.

Then the breeze died, and the light settled to a steady glow. Angelica glanced warmly at Jenna.

"I'm glad you girls came here tonight after all," she confided. "It's been so long since Julia and Hannah had visitors their own age. I'm sure they enjoyed it."

Jenna's mouth dropped open. What a strange thing to say!

Get away, she thought. Now. Get away from this woman as fast as you can. Losing her daughters has driven her mad.

"Uh, thanks," Jenna muttered, giving Hallie a nudge toward the door. "We'd better get going. Hallie's parents are surely wondering where we are."

"Wait," Angelica called.

Reluctantly, Jenna turned. Angelica stood in deep shadows now. Jenna could only see the ghostly gleam of her white clothing.

"You must come visit me at home sometime," she said. "We get terribly lonely, Simon and I. No one seems to be brave enough to call on the Fears. You girls, however, seem to have more courage than most. Please come. It would be so nice to have two girls around the house again. I do miss the laughter."

"Good night, Mrs. Fear," Jenna mumbled in answer.

She tugged at Hallie's arm and pulled her toward the doorway. Once outside, they started running. Jenna ran until her breathing rasped and her pulse beat like a hammer in her ears. She didn't look behind her until she passed the cemetery gates. Then she dared a single glance over her shoulder to make sure only Hallie was following her.

"Stop," Hallie panted, grabbing Jenna's arm. "I can't run anymore."

Jenna allowed herself to be pulled to a stop. She propped her hands on her knees and gasped for breath.

"Can you believe this?" Hallie asked.

"No," Jenna replied. "What a strange woman."

When bedtime came, Hallie lit a candle and led Jenna upstairs. The flickering circle of light surrounded them, moving up the stairs with them.

"Now, don't you girls spend the whole night talking," Mrs. Sheridan called from downstairs.

"We won't, Mother," Hallie replied. Dropping her voice to a whisper, she added, "Just most of it."

Her bedroom was tucked up beneath the eaves. Pretty, daisy-printed paper covered the walls. The curtains matched the yellow daisies, and yellow, green and white quilts covered the two narrow beds.

"You take the bed closest to the window," Hallie told Jenna.

Jenna sat down on the bed. With a yawn, she leaned back against the iron headboard. "Remember how we used to leap like frogs from bed to bed?" she asked.

"Do I ever," Hallie exclaimed. Her eyes sparkled. "Your mother was so angry the time we broke your bed!"

She sat down across from Jenna. Hallie picked up a brush from the nightstand and began brushing her hair. "Remember our Sister Oath? Let's do it again!"

"Hallie, we were six years old when we made that up."

"So what?" Hallie demanded.

Jenna smiled. "Oh, all right." Crossing her arms she reached out to take Hallie's right hand in her right, Hallie's left in her left. "We're sisters. We stand together, and protect each other. You for me and me for you. Forever."

"Forever," Hallie repeated.

They shook hands hard, then recrossed their arms and shook hands again. Jenna laughed. "Now let's get to bed."

Hallie blew the candle out. Darkness claimed the room, broken only by the faint moonlight sifting in through the window.

Jenna changed into her nightgown and slid under the covers. She felt exhausted. The long train ride, the scares in the graveyard, girls with no bones, Angelica Fear . . . Her eyelids drifted closed.

"Jenna?"

"Mmmm?"

"What do you think about the Fears?"

In the darkness behind her closed lids, Jenna called up the memory of Angelica Fear. So beautiful. And so strange. For a moment, the moldy, dead-flower smell of the graveyard wafted on the night air.

Jenna's breath caught in her throat. Then she shook her head. Her imagination had run away with her already tonight. She refused to let it happen again.

"I thought Mrs. Fear seemed strange," she said. "But I felt sorry for her, too. After all, she lost both her daughters. And as for that horrible story, well, I can't believe sisters would kill each other."

"You're not tempted, not even a little, to believe—"

"No," Jenna said firmly.

Hallie fell silent. Jenna felt herself drifting off to sleep.

"Jenna?"

"Yes, Hallie?" she mumbled.

"We're going to have to go visit the Fears, you know."

Jenna's eyes flew open. She sat up in bed. "Why?"

"Well, she invited us, for one thing."

The curtains belled in the breeze, sending shadows rippling across the ceiling. "I don't want to visit Angelica Fear," Jenna told her friend.

"Where's your spirit of adventure?" Hallie challenged.

"I think I used it all up tonight," Jenna retorted.

Hallie laughed. "Oh, come on, Jenna. Don't you want to see inside the Fears' house? I'll bet no one from town has been inside there in years."

"And probably with good reason, Hallie," Jenna retorted.

"You're honestly not the least bit curious?" Hallie prodded.

"No, I'm honestly not," Jenna insisted. Though she

secretly knew that she did feel curious. More than a little, actually.

Hallie's feather mattress rustled as she shifted position. "Jenna, you know I wasn't exactly truthful when I said I liked it here. I haven't made a single friend."

"Oh, Hallie, you will."

"I've tried my best," Hallie complained. "I'm an outsider here. The girls are polite, but none of them ever come to call. Sometimes I think I'll never fit in."

"What has this got to do with the Fears?" Jenna asked.

"Look, I'm not that eager to go there, either," Hallie confided. "But I have to. You see, no one else in town has ever dared to even walk up to the front door, no less gone inside their house. If we go, then all the other girls will want to hear about it. This is my chance to make friends."

"Oh, Hallie."

"Please?" the other girl pleaded.

Jenna wanted to refuse, but she couldn't. Hallie was her best friend. If going to the Fear house would make it easier for her to make friends here in Shadyside, then Jenna had to help.

"All right," she muttered. "I'll go with you. But just this once."

"You're the best sister any girl could have," Hallie vowed. "The very best."

"Now, *please* may I go to sleep?" Jenna begged.

Hallie laughed. "I didn't realize I was keeping you up. Yes, Jenna. Go to sleep."

With a sigh, Jenna closed her eyes. Slowly, the world began to fade away. She wasn't asleep, exactly.

Yet, hazy dreamlike images filled her mind. Pale shapes flitting through the night sky. Ghostly robes billowing out, drifting with the beat of wings.

A faint noise outside pulled her back to wakefulness. For a moment she lay still, listening. She heard the noise again.

What was that?

She heard it once more. Louder. Closer. The soft rustling sound made Jenna sit bolt upright in bed. Jenna's skin crawled as she realized what had made the eerie sound.

Wings.

Something big, taking flight. Swooping across the night sky.

Chapter
4

"Hallie!" Jenna whispered. "Hallie, wake up."

She heard her friend mumble. Then watched as Hallie rolled over and pressed her head deeper into her pillow. Jenna struggled to get up. She tiptoed over to the window. Beneath the sheltering branches, the woods looked dark and shadowy.

Not a single ray of moonlight intruded there.

Jenna stared intently at the woods. Nothing moved. Then a pale shadow darted out of the gloomy shadows beneath the trees.

It rose, flying over the woods. Then swooped straight at Jenna.

Pale, fluttering wings beat at the window. Claws screeched upon the glass. Jenna caught one horrified glimpse of round, staring eyes and a deformed mouth, opening and closing. Opening and closing.

With a cry, she jerked backward. Her knees caught

the edge of the bed, sending her down to the floor with a thump.

"What is it?" Hallie cried, surging up in bed.

"The . . . the window!" Jenna gasped.

Hallie rose and went to the window. "I don't see anything," she murmured sleepily. "Oh! Now I see it!" she added in a startled tone. She took a step back from the window and looked over at Jenna.

It took every bit of Jenna's courage to get up and return to the window. But she had to see. She had to know. Her pulse pounded in her ears as she looked out.

A white shape floated on the breeze. The long feathers of its wings splayed out as it spiraled down in a long glide. Then it swooped up again, something small and limp clutched in its claws. Tufts of feathers stood up like ears.

"That must be the biggest owl I've ever seen," Hallie remarked as she stumbled back to bed. "Looks like it caught a mouse for dinner."

Jenna's breath went out in a sigh of relief. A barn owl! Hunting down a field mouse. How silly could she be? She trembled with sheer relief as she climbed back into bed.

After the day she'd had today, a visit to the Fears should be easy as pie.

The hulking Fear mansion stood at the top of a low rise. Three stories tall, it rested on a foundation of blackish-green stone. A blanket of thick, dark ivy crawled over the stone, and up and over rows of dark-brown bricks. Curling around the arched windows and doorways, the ivy crept nearly to the second story.

A long, curved stone stairway and two tall turrets on either side of the house reminded Jenna of a castle in a fairy tale. A castle under an evil spell. A peaked gray roof and a tall, spindly chimney added to the unsettling impression.

A huge oak tree in the front yard hung low over the house. It was dying. Its leafless, skeletal limbs stretched towards the slate roof like bony, out-stretched arms. Almost as if it wanted to drag the house into death with it.

"This place is creepy," Hallie breathed.

"I'll say. Are you sure you want to do this?" Jenna asked.

Her friend shot her a glance with dancing blue eyes. "I wouldn't miss it for the world."

Jenna's legs felt rubbery as she climbed up the stone steps to the shadowy porch. A brass knocker hung in the center of the front door. Jenna couldn't tell what it was supposed to be. An animal of some kind, she thought. A lion or a tiger, maybe?

Then she saw that the tongue was forked like a snake's. It curled out from between long, pointed fangs. Jenna's stomach churned with distaste.

"Go ahead and knock," Hallie whispered.

"You," Jenna countered.

"You're closer."

Jenna took hold of the knocker and tried to lift it. For a moment, it felt as if it resisted her touch. She lifted harder. Then it came loose, so suddenly that she banged her knuckles on the creature's forehead.

Bongggg. The metallic clatter echoed through the house. Jenna let the knocker fall back into place and rubbed her skinned knuckles.

Suddenly, the door swung open.

Jenna could see nothing but shadows within. Dark. Thick.

She took a deep breath. Her throat had gone tight, and her skin felt cold despite the warm summer air.

Who had opened that door?

A pale oval appeared in the dimness. A face, Jenna realized. A man's face, hard and sharp. And ugly. Almost grotesquely so, Jenna thought as a wave of revulsion coursed through her body. Two black pits for eyes, jutting cheekbones, a slash of a mouth . . . She jumped in alarm as Hallie grabbed her by the arm.

"Jenna, who is that?" Hallie whispered.

Jenna could only shake her head. The face came closer. Two smaller patches of paleness seemed to float out of the shadows. His hands, Jenna realized with a shock.

Soon she could make out the vague outline of his body. Her breath went out in a gasp. Oh, so that was it! His dark clothing had blended with the shadows, making his face and hands seem disembodied.

"What are you doing here?" His voice boomed down at them.

A feeling like sharp-clawed mouse feet scampered up Jenna's spine. She wished she could see the man's eyes, but they held the darkness like pits of shadow in his face. Terror winged its black way through her heart, and she forgot about Hallie's painful grip on her arm.

"Answer me," he commanded in that same deep, dead voice.

"Uh, we're here to visit Mrs. Fear," Jenna ventured.

Those dark pits turned to her. "No one visits here."

"Simon, darling, is that our guests?"

Angelica's voice came from a doorway at the rear of the foyer. She stepped into view, her cream-colored gown seeming almost to glow with a light of its own. Her hair had been pinned into a crown of raven braids. For a moment she looked like a young girl. Then she tilted her head, flashing that stripe of white hair.

"Guests?" Simon asked, glancing over his shoulder at his wife.

"These are the girls I met last night," she explained. "Remember? I told you all about them."

"Ah," he nodded. His dark brows rose and his eyes widened. "Those girls. I remember."

Something glinted in the murky, shadowed pools of his eyes. Something chilling, Jenna thought.

"Please forgive me for temporarily forgetting my manners, ladies," Simon Fear murmured as he pulled the door open wider. "Allow me to welcome you to our home."

Jenna saw sunlight flood into the foyer, erasing the eerie shadows that had hidden his deep-set eyes. She met his penetrating stare, then looked away.

His eyes chilled her. Close-set and black, they peered out at her from beneath discolored, lizardlike lids.

A black waistcoat and trousers draped his tall, thin figure. Above his stiff white collar, his face looked gaunt and angular, his yellowish skin tinged with an unhealthy pallor. A thin, jagged white scar trailed from the corner of his left eye down to his jawline. His long, hooked nose reminded her of a pointed beak. Combed straight back from his forehead, his black hair appeared slick and greasy. He wore no mustache, but large, bushy sideburns covered his hollow cheeks.

"Do come in," he invited.

Jenna felt a prickle at the back of her neck. Then she felt Hallie push her across the threshold.

The inside of the house felt cool, and a musty, moldy smell tickled her nose. Dark shadows shrouded every corner, from the deep-green curtains draped over every window to the black marble staircase that curved up to the second floor.

Jenna heard the sound of tiny bells. She looked up. A crystal chandelier, stirred by the breeze, tinkled overhead. Shards of rainbows twirling across the floor and walls as the breeze shook the prisms. Then Simon closed the door, plunging the room back into darkness.

"We're so glad you came," Angelica told them. "Come into the drawing room, and we'll see about getting some tea. And you must forgive the lack of light," Angelica murmured. "My eyes are very sensitive. The doctor gave me strict instructions just last week to keep the curtains drawn in the daytime. Simon and I know our way around so well that we rarely use the lamps."

It looked to Jenna as if the curtains hadn't been opened in years. Not just days.

"It's been so long since we've had visitors," Angelica told the girls. "I can't tell you how happy we are to have you. Isn't that so, Simon?"

"Absolutely, my love," he replied.

Jenna glanced over her shoulder at him. He seemed taller somehow as he strode along behind them. His face wore no expression. His eyes burned with a secret, dark fire. She could understand how some of those terrible rumors had started.

"Here we are," Angelica murmured, leading the way into the drawing room.

Jenna had never been in such a luxurious room before. She'd never seen such rich furnishings or thick carpets. Heavy curtains shrouded these windows, too, but a round stained-glass window high up on the south wall filtered a jewel-hued light into the room.

"Simon, dear, will you ring for tea?" Angelica asked as she sat on the sofa. She patted the cushions beside her. "Come, girls."

Simon tugged at an embroidered cord that hung in the far corner of the room. Then he sat on the chair opposite the sofa and studied his guests. "So, girls, why don't you tell me about yourselves?" he asked. "Hallie, I understand your family is new here in Shadyside?"

Hallie nodded. "My father is the new school-teacher."

"An admirable profession," Angelica commented. "And how do you like your new town?"

"It's all right, I suppose," Hallie replied. Then she surprised Jenna by adding, "I've found it a little hard to make friends."

Simon cocked his head to one side. Jenna saw his

thin neck crane out of his collar like a turtle's. "In time, my dear. In time. Shadyside is a small village, and it takes a while for these townsfolk to accept newcomers."

"In New Orleans, things would be very different," Angelica told them. "I could sponsor you girls in a coming-out party. There would be balls and banquets and the opera. Alas, there's nothing of the sort in Shadyside."

"New Orleans!" Awe darkened Hallie's eyes. "I've always wanted to go there."

Angelica sighed. "Ah, New Orleans was such a lovely place. But then we had to come here, and I thought this was a lovely place, too. I'd hoped we would be happy here, but then my girls . . ." Jenna saw her smile fade. Then she brightened. "Well, it *is* nice to have visitors for a change."

Jenna heard a knock on the door. Simon rose and answered it. Jenna tried to catch sight of a maid. But when he opened the door, she saw only a wooden tea cart set with china and plates piled high with scrumptious cakes. The silver teapot gleamed and the starched crowns of the napkins stood like palace guards around the plates.

Simon wheeled the cart into the room and left it in front of Angelica. "Well, what have we here to offer our guests?" Angelica asked. "Anything look tempting to you, girls?"

Jenna's mouth watered as she smelled the delicious aroma of fresh scones. Angelica fixed them each cups of tea and plates of cake. Soon, she and Hallie eagerly sipped sweet tea and nibbled on the most delicious pastries they'd ever tasted.

Jenna tried to remember her manners and eat in a ladylike fashion. But when Angelica offered her seconds, she couldn't resist.

"You seem to like the scones," Angelica observed.

"Yes, ma'am," Jenna agreed.

"They're delicious," Hallie added.

Angelica smiled. "I make them myself. I learned the trick from a Scottish maid I once had, years ago." Her smile faded. "My daughters used to love them. I could never bake enough. Sometimes they even squabbled over the last few crumbs. . . ."

For a moment, Jenna thought she saw a glimmer of tears in the woman's eyes. She felt sorry for Angelica. Yes, she might seem a bit strange sometimes. But, after all, she'd lost both her daughters.

Simon leaned forward. "I understand that you're only visiting here, Jenna."

"For the summer," she agreed. "Hallie and I are best friends, and it's been hard for us to live so far apart."

"They're as close as sisters," Angelica told him.

"Ah," he replied solemnly. "Like sisters."

He and his wife shared a look and a smile. Then Angelica turned to Jenna.

"And how do *you* like Shadyside, Jenna?" she asked.

"I haven't seen much of it since I arrived last night," Jenna replied.

Simon chuckled. "I heard you got quite a tour of the cemetery, however."

Jenna felt her cheeks grow warm. "Well . . ."

"It's all right, my dear," he assured her. "My wife and I know you were only curious, and that sheer high-spiritedness lured you into our daughters' resting place. We have never begrudged a young person a bit of . . . high spirits."

He and Angelica laughed. Jenna didn't understand the joke, but then, these were grownups.

"I wouldn't worry about making friends," Simon told them, still chuckling. "You're both so pretty . . . I'm sure the young men will soon be flocking around begging for a moment of your time."

Jenna studied them. Angelica didn't seem so strange anymore, and Simon no longer held that grim, forbidding look that had frightened her at first. She felt herself beginning to relax and enjoy herself. She felt surprised when Hallie set her plate aside and got up.

"We've got to go now," Hallie announced. "My parents will be wondering where we are."

"They don't know?" Simon asked.

Hallie's face turned scarlet. Jenna realized that Hallie was up to her old tricks. "Well . . ."

"Ah, so you didn't tell them you were coming to visit the strange, notorious Fears," Angelica said.

Still blushing, Hallie ducked her head.

"You don't have to be embarrassed, my dear," Simon assured her. "We're used to the things people say about us. We've even learned not to pay it any mind. I'm just glad you decided to come despite the rumors."

He rose. "Still, we can't have you getting into trouble. So, if it's time to go, you shall."

"First," Angelica murmured as she rose from her seat. "I'd like to show you something."

She glanced at Simon again, Jenna noticed. As if

silently requesting his permission, she felt. He nodded at her and she smiled.

"Come, girls," Angelica ordered with a wave of her hand. "Follow me."

The Fears led the girls down the dim hallway to the foyer, then up the curving stairway. At the top of the stairs, they turned down another dim, narrow corridor. Jenna felt an uneasy twinge in her stomach.

Finally, Angelica stopped and flung open a heavy oak door. Heavy curtains covered the windows, like the other rooms, Jenna noticed. But enough light remained for Jenna to see the room clearly. A bedroom, decorated all in blue. Angelica led them inside. Jenna paused at the four-poster, canopied bed, her gaze resting on a beautiful china doll that sat in a nest of frilly lace pillows. A silver comb and brush sat on the dresser. Colorful hair ribbons twined around the handle of the brush.

"Such a pretty room, don't you think?" Angelica asked.

"Oh, yes!" Hallie replied as her hand gently stroked a fancy dress that hung across the back of a chair.

This had to be one of their daughters' rooms, Jenna knew. One of their *dead* daughters. It looked to Jenna as if it had been kept exactly the way the girl had left it.

As if the Fears expected her to return at any minute.

Jenna gazed around curiously. She noticed a glass case full of dolls and moved toward it. Most of them looked like the china doll on the bed. Then Jenna saw a group on a lower shelf, a type of doll she'd never seen before. Made out of bits of rag and straw, the crude bodies looked twisted and distorted. One of them looked different. Long silver pins protruded from its limbs. Jenna gritted her teeth and looked away. Yet, the bizarre sight drew her gaze back again.

She noticed that the pins had large, rounded ends. She looked closer and saw that the ends were actually carved images of tiny skulls. A large red stain marked each place the pins stabbed the doll's body. Pins had even been stabbed through the eyes.

The sight made Jenna shudder. With a hard knot in her stomach, she quickly turned away.

"Our dear Hannah loved to collect dolls," Simon confided. "All types of dolls. She even made some herself. She was quite clever with her hands."

"Yes, very clever," Angelica repeated proudly.

"Those dolls on the bottom," Jenna asked in a halting voice. "Did Hannah make those?"

"Why, yes," Simon replied slowly. "When we lived down in New Orleans. For such a young person, she already knew a great deal about voo—"

"Doll-making," Angelica cut in abruptly. Jenna noticed her exchange an intense glance with her husband. Then she looked at Jenna and smiled. "It's quite an art, you know."

"Hallie, I'd like to show you something," Angelica called. She strolled over to the dresser, where she opened a drawer and removed a blue velvet box. She snapped open the box and held it out to Hallie. Jenna spotted a heart-shaped gold locket within.

"This belonged to my daughter, Hannah," Angelica explained as she held the necklace out to Hallie. The gold winked and shimmered in the dim light. "I'd like you to have it."

"Oh, it's beautiful," Hallie exclaimed. She quickly

slipped the gold chain over her head. "I love it! Thank you."

"It looks lovely on you," Angelica told her. "It should be worn by a young girl, not sitting forgotten in a drawer."

"And now for Jenna," Simon murmured.

He led them across the hall to another bedroom decorated all in rose. Pink rosebuds splashed across the wallpaper, and the quilted coverlet ranged in shades from palest blush to deep coral. Pottery bowls and vases, in all different shapes and sizes, covered the dresser.

Angelica leaned over and picked up a large, round bowl decorated with birds and flowers. "Julia was so artistic, too," she explained, running one fingertip around the edge of the bowl. "She made many beautiful things, as you can see."

"May I see it?" Hallie asked.

"Why, of course," Angelica replied. She handed Hallie the bowl and began pointing out the details in each little bird and flower. From across the room Jenna heard Hallie's appreciative sighs.

Jenna glanced around Julia's room. Would she find another case of hideous dolls? Or something just as awful? In the far corner of the room, on a wooden pedestal, Jenna spotted a tall, domed birdcage. The pretty cage stood empty. Julia must have kept a pet bird, Jenna thought, and her parents felt too sentimental to remove the empty cage.

Jenna's gaze dropped to the bottom of the cage, where she saw a pile of small white bones.

"Julia was a nature lover," Jenna heard Angelica murmur from somewhere right behind her.

Jenna turned and looked at her.

"She adored all kinds of creatures," Angelica added emphatically. "Big or small. Pretty. Or homely. 'All creatures under the sun have their purpose, Mother' she used to say. Remember, Simon?" Angelica asked.

"How very true, too," Simon asserted. "Now, Jenna," he announced. "We have something for you."

He turned and opened a painted wooden box on the dresser. Lifting the lid, he slipped out a bracelet of delicate crystal beads. "Here you are, dear," he said, holding it out. "This was Julia's favorite piece of jewelry."

"I know she would be pleased to see it worn by a pretty young girl like you," Angelica offered.

Jenna's skin crawled. She didn't want it. She didn't want to *touch* a dead girl's bracelet, let alone wear it. But she couldn't think of a way to refuse politely.

Slowly, reluctantly, she extended her hand.

"Thank you," she muttered.

Simon laid the bracelet in her palm. Jenna started to put it away in her pocket.

"Oh, no, you must wear it," Simon protested. "Here, let me put it on for you."

Plucking the bracelet from her hand, he slipped it around her wrist and fastened the gold catch.

"It looks pretty on you, Jenna," Hallie told her.

Jenna held her wrist up. The crystal beads caught the light, reflecting it in a rainbow glitter. She'd never seen such a pretty bracelet, she thought, turning her arm from side to side. The glass beads felt cool against her skin, but soon picked up the heat from her body.

Then the bracelet got warmer.

That's impossible, she thought. She glanced at

Hallie. The other girl peered into a mirror, admiring her new necklace. Jenna saw nothing but pleasure showing in her face.

The bracelet grew hotter.

The shimmering beads felt like a band of fire, dancing around her wrist. Jenna stared down at them, noticing a pulsing red light deep in the center of each crystal sphere. The color of a burning ember. She rubbed at her skin, expecting to see a red mark. Her skin looked totally normal, but it felt circled by blistering flames.

The fiery sensation lanced up her forearm. The intense heat spread across her shoulders and back.

Higher. Fiery fingers choking her neck. Hotter. Shooting into her skull. Jenna gripped the sides of her head and screamed.

Chapter
5

"Jenna! What is it, dear?" Angelica grasped Jenna's arm and held her upright. "Do you feel faint?"

Jenna lifted her head and managed to focus on the older woman's face. Angelica's brow looked creased with concern. An odd expression glittered in her green eyes. Jenna opened her mouth to speak. But she could barely sound a few choked, unintelligible words.

"My dear girl, what on earth is the matter?" Angelica exclaimed. She pressed her cool palm to Jenna's burning cheek. "Why, she's dreadfully overheated," she told Simon.

"She looks quite pale," Simon observed.

Yet, with Angelica's hand still pressed to her cheek, Jenna suddenly felt the heat vanish. She let her breath out with a gasp. Her arms and legs felt as though they'd turned to jelly, and she struggled to stand upright.

She couldn't believe this. She just couldn't believe it!

"I was burning," she whispered, more to herself than to the others. "Skin, blood, bones. Burning."

"Have you lost your wits?" Hallie demanded, staring at her with wide, surprised eyes. "You weren't burning. You were just standing there with your eyes popping out of your head."

Jenna shook her head. It had felt so real, so frightening. Now, she felt normal again. What was happening to her?

"I . . . don't understand," she whispered. She pulled away from Angelica's hold.

Simon and Angelica exchanged a look. "These rooms are so stuffy. You simply need some fresh air, my dear," Simon suggested. "Perhaps a glass of water?"

"Yes, that's it," Angelica agreed. "We should have thought to open the windows on such a warm day. How careless."

It *is* very hot up here, Jenna thought. She only needed some fresh air. Just because the bracelet had once belonged to a dead girl, she'd let her imagination run away with her again.

"Yes, I must have gotten too warm," she told Angelica and Simon. "That makes sense."

Hallie laughed. "Jenna likes things to make sense."

"Ah." Simon cocked one dark brow. "And you, Hallie? Do you like things to make sense?"

"I like adventure," she told him. "And I'm always getting poor Jenna in trouble."

"And why do you let Hallie get you into trouble, Jenna?" Simon asked curiously.

Jenna shrugged. "She's my best friend," she explained.

"And she'd never desert me in a pinch," Hallie added. "Right, Jenna?"

"Right," Jenna replied with a nod. Again, she noticed Simon and Angelica exchange a meaningful glance. Almost as if they were sending each other a silent message, Jenna felt. But that was impossible. As impossible as the burning bracelet.

"Jenna, are you sure you're feeling all right?" Angelica asked.

"I'm fine, honest," Jenna insisted.

Sure or not, she wanted to get out of this house as fast as possible. She shot a glance at Hallie. "We really have to be going now, Hallie."

Hallie blinked, almost as if she'd been daydreaming. "Oh. Yes. I suppose we do," she agreed.

"We'll show you to the door," Simon offered, leading the way.

Angelica strolled behind him. Jenna followed, pulling Hallie after her. Once again, the walk down the long, shadowy hallway felt endless.

Jenna paused, glancing down at her wrist. Even in the dim corridor, the crystal bracelet sparkled, as if lit from within.

She turned and followed Angelica and Hallie downstairs. Up ahead, she saw Simon opening the heavy front door.

"Thank you for coming to visit," he said, holding the door as they passed. "I hadn't realized how lonely we were until I saw your fresh young faces. Such pretty girls."

Hallie giggled. "Thank you."

"And you do remind me of sisters," he added, his cold, dark eyes fixing on Jenna.

"Thank you," she mumbled as she quickly stepped toward the threshold.

She felt Angelica's grip on her arm, stopping her dead in her tracks. Angelica's thin fingers felt very cool, her pointy nails biting into Jenna's flesh through the fabric of her gown.

"Promise you'll come again," Angelica urged. "I don't think I could bear it if you didn't."

"Of course we'll come again," Hallie vowed.

Astonished, Jenna stared at her friend. She couldn't believe Hallie had promised to return!

Hallie didn't seem to notice Jenna's stare. She led the way out onto the porch, pausing to wave to their hosts as she neared the steps. Jenna didn't look back. The moment they were out of sight of the house, she ripped off the bracelet.

"What are you doing?" Hallie demanded.

"I'm not going to wear this," Jenna replied.

"Why not?"

Jenna shuddered, remembering that terrifying moment when her body felt swallowed up by flames. "It belonged to a *dead* girl."

"So what?" Hallie retorted. "So did my locket, and I love it. I'm going to wear it all the time."

"Well, I can't."

Hallie laughed. "You're a goose, Jenna. It's such a pretty bracelet. The Fears were very generous to give it to you and you're making something horrible out of it."

"I don't feel right wearing it," Jenna insisted. "And I can't believe you promised to go back there."

"Why not?" Hallie asked. "Don't you feel sorry for them? Especially Angelica. I thought she would burst out crying when she told us the story about the scones."

"I thought so, too," Jenna replied. Jenna had never seen anyone look quite as mournful as Angelica did each time she spoke about her daughters. And she had felt sorry for her. Yet, sorry or not, some other voice whispered an urgent warning.

"Yes, I feel sorry for them," she told her friend. "And they were nice to us. But I don't want to go back."

"They might give us more pretty things," Hallie wheedled.

"Hallie, that's awful!"

The other girl tossed her blond curls. "Oh, you know I don't mean that. But the other girls are going to be *so* jealous when they find out we were invited here. And every time we go back, we'll have something exciting to tell our new friends."

Jenna pressed her hand against her pocket, feeling the hard shape of the crystal beads. "If that's the only reason they'd want to be your friends, maybe they're not worth having as friends."

"That's easy for you to say," Hallie retorted. "You can go back to Brentsville where you know everybody."

"Hallie—"

With a whirl of skirts and blond hair, Hallie spun around and started running toward the woods.

"Wait!" Jenna shouted after her. "Hallie, what are you doing? Hallie!"

But either Hallie didn't hear, or didn't pay attention. She kept running. A moment later, she disappeared among the trees. Jenna let her breath out in a hiss of exasperation.

"Well, suit yourself, Hallie. I'm not about to chase you all the way home," Jenna said aloud, feeling irritated with her friend. "I'm going to take my time . . . and you can just wait."

She set off toward the Sheridans' home. The sun sat low in the summer sky, illuminating the thick, green woods with slanting beams of red-orange light. Masses of tiny purple flowers carpeted the ground. They seemed to glow against the dark leaves that covered the forest floor.

Jenna felt her foul mood vanish. She knew Hallie. Once her friend ran off her temper, she'd be cheerful and agreeable again.

Jenna walked slowly and gazed around. The light changed from orange to deep red and it seemed as though she'd stepped inside a jewel. She spotted the nodding blooms of some Queen Anne's lace, and stopped to pick a bouquet.

Raising the flowers to her nose, she inhaled their scent as she strolled on. She'd give the flowers to Mrs. Sheridan. Hallie's mother would be pleased, Jenna decided.

Her foot slammed painfully into a tree root and her arms windmilled for a moment as she tried to keep her balance. The flowers flew in all directions as she hit the ground face forward. Hard enough to knock the wind out of her lungs.

Jenna lay gasping, her cheek pressed to the soft, damp floor of the woods. Finally, she took a deep breath and started to push herself up. Her right hand slipped out from under her and she felt something sticky on her palm. Ugh! She sat quickly and stared down at her hand.

"What—" she began.

A dark smear stained her palm.

Mud. Yuck. She rubbed her hand on her dress.

No. Not mud.

A red, wet stain marked the pale-yellow fabric of her dress.

Jenna stared down at the crimson smear. A bitter taste flooded the back of her throat.

Blood.

Chapter 6

Jenna scrambled to her feet. She must have cut herself. Badly, too, to be bleeding so much. She searched her palm, but didn't find a wound. Strange, her hand didn't hurt at all, either.

It didn't make sense. Why didn't she see a cut? Where did the blood come from?

A chill slithered up her spine. If this wasn't her blood, then it must be . . . someone else's.

Her gaze dropped to the spot on the forest floor where she had fallen.

All around, thick, red splotches coated the green leaves. Jenna had never seen so much blood. She took a step backward. Blood spattered the ground and dripped down the trunk of a white birch tree. With a gasp, she stared in shock at the bloody handprint that stood out with terrible sharpness against the white bark.

Just above the handprint, a thin metal object glinted in the fading sunlight. Like a silver knitting needle jabbed into the tree.

Jenna reached out and yanked the metal object by its rounded, knobby end. She looked down at it. Her lip curled back in horror. A small, carefully carved skull stared up at her from the needle's rounded end. The other end tapered to a fine, incredibly sharp tip.

Jenna knew instantly what she held in her hand.

The long silver pin looked exactly like those she'd seen at the Fears' house: the pins that stabbed through the hideous doll made by Hannah Fear.

She swiftly glanced back at the blood-splattered tree and ground. Then down at the silver, skull-headed needle that glistened with droplets of blood.

Jenna shrieked in horror and flung the needle onto the ground.

She heard the underbrush rustle. Then the unmistakable crunch of footsteps on the path nearby.

Who was out there? The person who had left that bloody print on the tree . . . and that horrifying silver needle?

He'd seen her. He was coming back.

Jenna felt her breath coming in heavy gasps. She had to run. Get away. Fast. But her feet felt rooted to the ground.

A scream welled up in her chest. She fought to swallow it back. But couldn't.

Her shriek echoed through the woods.

Whirling, she started running. She ran and ran. Down the narrow, twisting path and then into the dark woods.

Close behind her, she heard the footsteps, faster now. Pounding on the forest floor.

She picked up her skirt and ran with one arm out to push back the scratching branches that blocked her way. She crashed through the tangled brush and low-lying tree boughs. Her skirts tangled in her legs, and branches clawed at her hair as she tore through the bushes. Her hair fell loose from her braid and whipped wildly across her face.

Still, the footsteps followed her.

She ran faster than she'd ever run in her life. Her heartbeat roared in her ears. Each breath burned her chest and her legs ached painfully. But she kept going. Thinking of the blood. The long silver needle. Dripping with blood.

Her toe caught on a tree root and she stumbled to the ground. Exhausted, she desperately pulled herself up and staggered forward. She couldn't fall. She couldn't stop.

Not now. Not here.

She stilled her breath and listened.

The footsteps still followed. Closer and closer.

No! a voice in Jenna's mind roared. She couldn't let him catch her, she couldn't.

She heard the footsteps even louder now. She kept moving forward. But the woods grew so thick here. She could barely take a step without her feet tangling in vines and stiff, scratchy bushes.

He was right behind her. She could hear his breath rasping nearly as fast as hers.

She wasn't going to make it. He was faster, stronger. He was going to get her.

A sob of despair rose in her throat as she clawed her way through the brush.

"No," she panted. "No!"

She felt two heavy hands grab her shoulders. She struggled to pull away, but the grip felt too strong.

Twisting and struggling, she screamed with all her might.

Her shriek of sheer horror rang through the dark woods.

But she knew no one could hear her. No one could help her.

Jenna's captor wrapped a powerful arm around her waist and pulled her to a stop.

Chapter
7

"Let me go!" Jenna cried, struggling frantically.

Her captor held on, impossibly strong. She squirmed and struggled, bruising herself in his grasp.

"Stop," a low voice murmured in her ear. "Don't be afraid."

Taking her by both shoulders, he turned her around to face him. Jenna found herself looking up at a boy around her own age. He stood at least a head taller than her. Dark-brown hair flopped across his broad forehead. Jenna stared into his deep brown eyes.

"Don't hurt me," she gasped.

He kept his grip on her shoulders, but his touch felt gentle. "I'm not going to hurt you," he assured her. "I promise."

"Y-you chased me."

"I heard you screaming," he explained. "I only wanted to help."

She saw only kindness in his dark eyes. Kindness and concern. He smiled at her and she felt herself calming down a bit.

"Just get your breath back and tell me what happened."

"I was walking back there somewhere," she started to explain. "I tripped and fell to the ground. Right into a puddle of blood."

His eyes widened. "Blood?"

"All over," she cried, her voice high and strange-sounding. "On the ground and the leaves. And up on a tree trunk, someone had left a bloody handprint . . ."

She noticed that he stared down at her skirt. She glanced down, and gasped. An ugly crimson streak stained the fabric where she had rubbed her hand. Her stomach bucked and heaved.

"Now, calm down," he soothed.

"I *am* calm," she insisted.

Only then did she realize that she was trembling so badly that her teeth chattered. She fought for control. Finally, she managed to stop the shudders.

"Look, you don't have to talk about it anymore. Why don't I take you home?" he offered.

"No—" Jenna shook her head. "There's more. Something else."

He peered at her. "What do you mean?"

"When I looked closer, I found this long, silver needle. Stuck in the tree," Jenna stammered. "One end was pointed and the other had a silver skull carved on it."

"Silver needles? I don't understand," he gazed at her with a puzzled expression. Did he think she'd made it all up?

"It's hard to explain what they look like," Jenna

explained. She stared down at her ruined dress again and twisted a bit of fabric in her hand.

Should she tell this stranger about the dolls she'd seen at the Fears' house? No, probably not. If he lived in the village and heard she'd been visiting the Fears, he'd have even more reason to doubt her strange story. He might leave her alone right here and now. Jenna knew she couldn't stand being left alone in these woods right now.

"I'm sorry," Jenna stammered and looked up at him again. "I guess you can just believe me or not. I did see all this blood and this long, silver pin. Like an incredibly sharp knitting needle. Stabbed into the tree."

He studied her for a moment. "Did you see anything else? An animal carcass, maybe? You might have simply stumbled on a place where a hunter had shot and dressed a rabbit or a deer."

"I didn't see anything like that," Jenna shook her head. An animal wounded by a hunter might have left the blood. But what about the skull-tipped needle? Now she wished she'd taken it with her, at least to show Hallie.

"Do you want me to go look?" the boy asked.

It sounded like a logical way to prove her story. He could go see it all for himself. But when Jenna glanced around, her heart dropped.

"I . . . I can't tell you how to get there." She sighed and glanced around the darkening woods. "I ran off the path and stumbled around so much, I have no idea what direction I came from."

"And I was so intent on catching you that I didn't pay attention to where I was going," he replied.

He raked his hair back with one hand. "I'm sure that whatever you saw was frightening," he told her kindly. "But it sounds to me like you stumbled upon a spot where a hunter shot and dressed a deer."

"But there was so much blood!" she protested.

"A deer is a large animal," he pointed out. "And if the hunter dressed it there, he was bound to have blood on his hands."

A deer. A hunter. It all made sense. Jenna could almost believe his reasonable-sounding words. If she didn't stop to think about the ominous silver pin.

But what good would it do to stand here arguing about it? She couldn't even explain it to herself.

"You're right," she agreed finally. "It must have been a hunter."

"Just to be sure, I'll come back tomorrow and look for the spot in daylight. All right?"

Jenna eagerly nodded. "Yes. All right."

"Good. Now let me take you home. I'm sure your family is wondering where—"

"Oh, no!" Jenna gasped. "Hallie!"

Seeing the confusion on the boy's face, she hurried to explain. "Hallie's my friend. She ran away just to tease me, and that's why I was in the woods alone. Now, I'm sure she'll be worried about me."

"Then we'll get you home," the boy said. "Do you live in town?"

"I don't live around here. I'm visiting Hallie's family for the summer. They live on the eastern edge of town. On Crescent Lane."

"Then we ought to walk this way," he said, pointing straight ahead.

Straightening her shoulders, she pushed her tousled hair back behind her ears. "My name is Jenna Hanson, by the way."

"My name is Rob," the boy said, falling into step beside her. "Rob Smith."

In the lingering light of the setting sun, Jenna studied Rob from the corner of her eye. He was about her age, or maybe a couple of years older. Even though she'd just met him, she liked him very much. His eyes had a gentle look, and his smile seemed honest and open.

"Have you ever been to Shadyside before?" he asked.

"This is my first visit," she replied. "Hallie and I used to live in the same town in Virginia, but her family moved here a few months ago."

"You're a good friend to come all that way for a visit. I guess you missed her a lot," he replied.

"I did. I don't have any brothers or sisters. Neither does Hallie. So we're really close. What about you?" she asked. "Do you have any brothers or sisters?"

"I . . ." His voice caught oddly. "No."

"Do you live in Shadyside?"

A frown rumpled his forehead. "Uh, no. I came here a . . . a while ago. The Fears hired me as their handyman and groundskeeper, and even let me use the gardener's cottage on their estate."

The Fears? He worked for the Fears? At the mere mention of their name, Jenna felt icy fingertips race across her scalp.

She glanced at Rob. His steps had slowed and he gazed around the woods, looking confused. Did he think that they were lost?

"Rob, is anything wrong?" she asked. "We're not lost again or anything, are we?"

"Uh, no. We're not lost. We'll come to the edge of the woods in just a few minutes. The road to your friend's house meets the woods right at that point," he promised. He glanced at her, then looked away.

They walked along in silence for a few moments. "Where are you from?" she asked, picking up the conversation again.

"I . . ." He turned to look at her, then looked away. His eyes looked strange. Glassy and pained. As if trying to answer her had somehow caused him extreme discomfort.

"I . . . I'm from . . . from . . ." he stammered. His voice sounded choked.

He raised his hand to his throat as his mouth opened and closed. But Jenna heard no words come out. Alarm stabbed like a red-hot blade through Jenna's chest. Something was wrong, terribly wrong!

"Rob?" she whispered.

He staggered. With one hand, he grabbed a nearby sapling. With the other, he grabbed Jenna's sleeve. Jenna saw fear and confusion in his eyes. And a plea for help.

She didn't know what to do. She gripped his arms as his legs sagged beneath him.

"Rob!" she cried. "Don't fall! Please don't fall!"

His eyes rolled back in his head. Then he dropped in a heap on the forest floor.

Jenna crouched down beside him. "Rob!"

He didn't answer. Didn't move. She stared down at his white, still face. Her pulse drummed in her ears. She laid her palm on his chest, searching for his heart.

No heartbeat.

No sign of breath.

"No," she whispered, her mind reeling. It couldn't be! A moment ago, he'd been walking beside her. Talking. Smiling. He couldn't be. . . .

Dead.

Chapter
8

Jenna touched Rob's face. She slapped his cheek. "No, please. Wake up, Rob," she whispered.

She stared down at Rob, searching for some tiny sign of movement.

Tears blurred her vision. She dashed them away with the back of her hand. Her mind raced. The Fears, the blood, the long silver needles. Her terrifying flight through the woods. It all seemed like a bad dream.

"Rob," she whispered. "Rob, please wake up. You have to!"

His dark eyes slowly opened. He peered up at her and squinted. Jenna gasped with relief. She sat back and took a deep breath.

"I . . . blacked out again," he muttered. He rubbed his hand over his eyes.

Jenna felt as though the whole world had taken a

spin. "I thought . . . I thought . . ." She couldn't finish it. "This has happened before?"

He pushed himself to a sitting position. Color began to fill his cheeks and lips, replacing the ghastly paleness.

"A few times," he confided. "I can't seem to remember anything about my life before I came here. And when I try, it's as though a vise clamps down on my head, and everything turns black."

"Did you fall or hit your head?" Jenna asked.

"I can't remember."

"Do you have friends, a family?"

He scrubbed at his face with his hand. "I can't remember. I can't remember *anything,*" he replied in a bleak tone.

Jenna's heart ached for him. Without thinking, she reached out and put her hand on his arm. "Well, you have a friend now," she told him. Then she blushed, embarrassed by her own forwardness.

His eyes widened with surprise. Then he smiled at her. "Thanks," he murmured.

Jenna knew what it was like to be lonely. After Hallie had moved away, it felt as if her whole world had become empty. She couldn't imagine how Rob felt, alone in the world and unable to remember anything about his past.

"Can you walk?" she asked.

"Sure. Once the blackness passes, I'm as good as new," he replied.

He rose to his feet, pulling Jenna up with him. They set off again toward the Sheridans' house. The sun had set and Jenna noticed a few twinkling stars sprinkled across the night sky.

A few minutes later, they stepped out onto the road. Jenna recognized the spot. She turned to the left and spotted the roof of the Sheridans' house. Through the trees, she saw a light shining in the kitchen window.

"There it is," she said, pointing. "I should go in now."

"Are you sure you don't want me to come the rest of the way?" Rob asked.

"I'm sure," Jenna replied. "I—"

A loud rustling in the bushes dried up the words in her throat. Gasping, she turned toward the noise. She couldn't see anything in the shadowy undergrowth, however. Twigs popped and crackled as something big pushed through them.

"What is it?" she whispered.

Rob stepped in front of her. "I don't know. Run to the house. I'll deal with this."

"And leave you here alone?" she cried. "I will not!"

"Jenna—"

"No. I won't leave," she insisted.

The crackling grew louder. Closer. Jenna's knees felt weak and her heart beat so loud, she thought it would beat right out of her chest. Still, she didn't turn and run toward the house.

Jenna bent and picked a large stick up from the ground. Not much of a weapon, she knew. She gripped the stick so hard her hands hurt. The time for running had passed.

It was here.

Chapter
9

"Jenna! Where in the world have you been?"

Hallie's voice burst out of the bushes. Jenna felt so surprised that she dropped her stick.

"Hallie?" she quavered. "Is that you?"

"No, goose, it's the Queen of England."

Hallie pushed through the last section of bushes and stepped out onto the road. She shot Jenna an icy glare.

"Where have you been?" Hallie demanded. "I thought you'd gotten lost. I thought you'd fallen and broken your leg or something. Do you realize I've been trudging through miles of woods looking for you?"

Rob turned to look at Jenna. A huge grin stretched across his face.

"I thought it must be a bear," he said.

"Or maybe a mountain lion," Jenna added with a laugh.

"Thanks a bunch," Hallie groused. "And who are you?" she asked Rob. She stared at him suspiciously.

"This is Rob Smith," Jenna explained before he could answer. "He found me in the woods when I got lost. I fell and . . ."

"Jenna, what's that stain on your dress?" Hallie asked with a gasp. She stared down at Jenna's skirt. "It looks like . . . blood! Did you hurt yourself?" she asked.

"I'm fine," Jenna assured her friend. "But I stained my dress when I fell. I landed in a big puddle of blood."

Hallie shuddered and squeezed her eyes shut. "Yuck! That's disgusting!" Then she reached out and squeezed Jenna's hand. "You must have been terrified."

"Pretty much," Jenna admitted with a shrug. She wanted to tell Hallie about the silver needle she'd seen there, too. But she decided to wait.

"I think it might have been where a hunter dressed a deer," Rob explained. "Anyway, I'm going to go back in the morning and see. What were *you* girls doing in the woods?"

"We were coming back from visiting the Fears." Hallie reached up and stroked the locket Angelica had given her.

"I work for the Fears," Rob told her.

"Do you like them?" Hallie asked.

"They're all right."

Hallie glanced at him from under her lashes. "Haven't you heard the rumors about the creepy noises that come from the house at night, and the way their dead daughters walk the graveyard at night?"

"Hallie!" Jenna exclaimed.

"It's all right, Jenna," Rob replied. "I don't go into town much, Hallie. I don't know the Fears all that well. But they gave me a job and a place to stay when I needed both, and that's enough for me."

"I was just teasing," Hallie replied lightly. "I don't really believe all those crazy stories anyway. Especially after meeting the Fears," she added, still rubbing the locket. "Jenna, we'd better get back. Mother and Father will be wondering what happened to us."

"So long, Jenna," Rob said. "I'm glad we met. It's good to have a friend."

"Bye, Rob," Jenna waved as he strode away. As she watched him disappear into the shadows, she felt Hallie close beside her.

"He's very good-looking," Hallie whispered. "Are you sweet on him?"

"Oh, Hallie! There you go," Jenna replied, shaking her head. Hallie could conjure up a romance out of thin air. Jenna liked Rob. But she didn't feel anything more than friendship for him.

"He's just a friend," Jenna replied. "Honest."

Hallie shot her a look from under her lashes. "Now, tell me again about the blood."

Jenna told her the whole story. This time, she even told Hallie about the long silver pin. But Hallie didn't seem to understand what Jenna was talking about.

"Maybe you found something hunters use when they skin and dress a deer," Hallie offered.

"I don't think so," Jenna replied slowly. "It looked

just like the pins in those weird dolls that the Fears showed us."

"What dolls?" Hallie asked. Jenna thought Hallie must be teasing her. Until she noticed the confused look on Hallie's face.

"You know, those ugly cloth dolls that sat on the bottom of the glass case in Hannah Fear's bedroom?" Jenna reminded her. "One of them had long silver pins sticking into it. Simon Fear told us that Hannah had made them herself," Jenna reminded her.

Hallie still stared back at her with a blank, puzzled expression. "I must have missed that," she replied. "I don't remember seeing anything like that at the Fears' house."

Jenna felt confused. And frustrated. The one person in the world she wanted to confide in didn't know what she was talking about.

"Don't you believe me?" Jenna demanded.

Hallie stared at her wide-eyed. Her fingers twisted and pulled on her golden heart locket. "Of course I believe you," she protested. "I believe that you saw the blood. For goodness' sake, there's that big stain on your dress. And I believe that you saw something stuck into a tree, some long, sharp, metal . . . something," Hallie added. "But—"

"But what?" Jenna challenged her.

"Well, I'm just wondering if you really looked that closely at the dolls. I mean, the rooms were dark, Jenna."

She didn't understand why, but Jenna could tell Hallie didn't believe her. Had she really forgotten things that they both saw at the Fears' house?

As they walked toward the Sheridans', Hallie just smiled at her. And still, her fingers moved on the smooth surface of the locket.

Rubbing and rubbing and rubbing.

Jenna opened her eyes as bright streaks of sunlight streamed into Hallie's room through the flowered curtains. She yawned and rubbed her eyes. Then she glanced over at the other bed. Hallie lay on her back, her chest rising and falling with deep, regular breathing.

"Hallie?" Jenna whispered.

No answer.

"Wake up, Hallie," Jenna called, louder this time. "Time to get up."

Still, Hallie didn't respond. Strange. Hallie always sprang out of bed, eager for the day. Was her friend feeling sick today?

Jenna rose and padded over to the other bed. Hallie's eyelids fluttered. She breathed heavily, still deeply asleep. The locket lay in the hollow of her throat. It twitched with the rhythm of her heartbeat.

The chain looked a bit tight around Hallie's neck. Jenna reached out to rearrange it. The moment she touched it, however, Hallie's eyes flew open. Her hand shot out, grabbing Jenna's wrist in an unbearably tight grip.

"Ow!" Jenna yelped.

"What are you doing?" Hallie demanded.

"Fixing your chain," Jenna explained, stunned by her friend's action.

"Oh." After a moment, Hallie let her go. Then she sat up, rubbing the sleep from her eyes. "You startled me."

"Sorry," Jenna muttered. She rubbed her wrist.

"We have to go back to the Fears'," Hallie announced.

Jenna blinked in astonishment. "What?"

"We have to go back." A faraway look came into Hallie's eyes. Her hand crept up to touch the locket. "They were nice to us. And they don't have any other friends. Don't you feel the least bit sorry for them, Jenna?"

"Hallie—"

She broke off as someone rapped sharply on the door. "Time to get up, sleepyheads," Mrs. Sheridan called. "Did you forget about the barn raising at the Miller farm?"

"The barn raising!" Hallie exclaimed. "I forgot all about it."

"What's a barn raising?" Jenna asked.

Hallie tucked the locket beneath her nightgown. Her fingertips lingered at the spot where it rested, just over her heart.

"Here in Shadyside, when someone needs a barn, they invite all their neighbors over," she told Jenna. "All the men work together to build the barn, the women cook, and then everyone has a wonderful picnic. Father says they'll even play music and dance."

"Oh, that sounds like fun!" Jenna exclaimed.

Hallie nodded. Then a mischievous smile curved her lips. "This is the time to tell the other girls that we went to visit the Fears. They'll be *dying* to hear all the details."

Mr. Sheridan drove them all to the Millers' in the carriage. Carriages, wagons and horses crowded the lawn. It seemed as though the whole town of Shadyside had come to the barn raising. Heaps of lumber had been brought in from the sawmill. And Jenna saw long tables covered with cloths where the food would be served.

The skeleton of the barn had already been built, and men clambered all over it. The air rang with the sound of hammers and saws. A haze of sawdust hung over everything and the scent of new wood permeated the air.

Mr. Sheridan rolled up his shirtsleeves, then left to join the other men.

Mrs. Sheridan lifted a picnic basket out of the wagon. She handed it to Hallie. "You girls take this into the house for me," she said. "Then you can run and join the rest of the young people."

"I can't wait!" Hallie exclaimed with a laugh.

Her voice sounded higher than usual, and there was a breathlessness in it that made Jenna glance curiously at her friend. What is going on with her? she wondered. Maybe she really did feel ill today but didn't want to miss out on the party.

She helped Hallie carry the heavy basket into the house. A harried, red-faced woman took it from them, then shooed them back out into the sunshine.

"Now, where—" Hallie broke off suddenly, then pulled Jenna around to face another direction. "Look! Isn't that your beau?"

Jenna saw Rob coming toward them. "He isn't my beau," she protested. "He's my friend."

Hallie laughed, that same high-pitched giggle that Jenna had heard before. The sound made her uneasy. But then Rob called her name, distracting her from worries about Hallie.

"How are you, Jenna?" he asked, stopping in front of her.

Before she could answer, Hallie stepped in front of her. "Why, hello, Rob," she greeted him. "I didn't know we'd be seeing you again today."

Rob blinked, obviously surprised. "Hello, Hallie. How are you?"

"Perfect," she murmured. "You know, you look even taller today, Rob, than you did last night. And you've got the widest shoulders! Jenna, did you notice?"

"Uh—" Jenna muttered. She wanted to sink right into the ground and never come up again.

Her shrill giggle made Jenna's teeth stand on edge. What was wrong with Hallie? She never acted like this.

"Don't mind her," Hallie murmured as she stood closer to Rob. "She isn't used to talking to boys."

Why, she's flirting with him! Jenna thought. She couldn't believe it! Obviously, neither could Rob. He stared at Hallie as if he thought she'd lost her mind.

"I'd better get back to the barn," he mumbled. Shooting a glance at Jenna, he added, "See you later."

Jenna watched him stride away. Then she swung around toward her friend. "Hallie, what on earth is the matter with you today?" she demanded. "I've never seen you act that way—with a boy or anyone else."

"There they are!" Hallie exclaimed, as though Jenna hadn't said anything at all.

Without a further word, she straightened her bonnet and merrily skipped away. Jenna stared after her, and saw that she was headed toward a group of girls who stood talking in the shade of a big maple tree.

Jenna went after her friend. Hallie was in a very

strange mood, and she needed someone to watch out for her.

Hallie marched right up to the girls. "Hi," she said. "I'm Hallie Sheridan. This is my friend Jenna Hanson."

The other girls stared curiously for a moment. Then they all offered their names. Jenna lost track. Kate and Melissa and Jane, and she thought the redheaded one was named Francie. They seemed nice.

"Jenna and I have been exploring Shadyside," Hallie announced.

"Really?" one of the girls asked. "Have you been to see the old flour mill down near the river? It's very pretty there."

"Not yet." Hallie laughed, and there was a frantic glitter in her eyes that Jenna didn't like at all. "But we did go visit the Fears."

Dead silence was the only reply Jenna heard to Hallie's remark. Jenna watched as the girls' faces drained of color.

"You . . . visited them?" the redheaded girl asked at last. "You went inside their house?"

Hallie nodded. "They're very rich, you know. The house is full of expensive things, and they even gave us gifts. Some of their daughters' jewelry."

"Oh, look, there's Frank Douglas," one of the girls said, pointing toward a tall young man near the barn. "I simply have to talk to him!"

"We'll come with you," the redheaded girl offered.

The whole group walked away. The redheaded girl glanced over her shoulder once, and Jenna saw fear in her eyes. Real fear.

On one hand, she felt sorry for the Fears. They'd lost

both their daughters, and had been shunned by their neighbors. On the other hand, the very mention of their name struck terror into the people of this town.

Why? What could have happened here to make the townsfolk fear Simon and Angelica so?

"This is all your fault!" Hallie snapped.

Jenna turned to her, completely taken aback. "What? What are you talking about?"

"If you hadn't come with me, I would have made friends with those girls."

For a moment, Jenna was too astonished to reply. Hallie thrust her face close. Her normally laughing blue eyes looked hard with anger.

"I worked so hard to make friends here," she said. "It's been so hard. But you come waltzing in here and make a friend the very first day. Then the minute I make some progress, you ruin it for me!"

Jenna couldn't believe it. Her friend, her best friend, had turned on her. And for no reason! Jenna couldn't understand it.

"I didn't do anything to you!" she protested. "I hardly said a thing to those girls. It was the Fears. They got scared when you mentioned visiting the Fears."

"They were not!" Tears leaked from Hallie's eyes. She didn't seem to notice that she was crying.

Jenna's outrage vanished at the sight of those tears. Something was wrong with Hallie, and fighting with her wasn't going to do any good.

"Hallie, you've been acting strange all day," she whispered, anxious to help her friend. "First, you scared me silly when I tried to touch that locket this morning, and then you flirted with Rob, and now this—"

"I can't talk to you right now," Hallie cried, flinging her hands up. "I wish you hadn't come here. I wish something awful would happen to these people. I wish . . . I wish that whole stupid barn would just fall down around their heads!"

Whirling, she walked off. Jenna stared after her, unsure what to think or do. There had been such anger in Hallie's face, such malice in her eyes. It was as if she'd suddenly become a different person overnight.

"I wonder what's the matter with her," she muttered.

She scanned the crowd for Hallie, but the other girl seemed to have vanished into thin air. Frustrated, she turned one way, then the other.

Her gaze drifted to the barn. She could see Rob, high up on the roof. He and Frank Douglas and two other men hammered on timbers at the very peak.

A shadow fell across the barn. A faint shadow. Very faint. But the sight of it sent Jenna's nerves tingling with alarm. She glanced up at the sky.

Nothing. Not a single cloud to mar the pure stretch of blue.

She looked at the barn again. The shadow seemed to twine around the skeletal framework like a gossamer snake. No one else seemed to notice. She shook her head, denying her own senses.

Then the barn trembled.

Jenna took a step forward, then stopped. The sun shone down gaily. Everyone else chatted and laughed, even the men working on the barn. No one seemed to see the shadow. No one seemed to have noticed the building's faint shiver.

For a moment, Jenna thought she might have somehow lost her mind.

Then another, sharper tremor passed through the framework. This time, however, some of the workers noticed it, too. Several of the men on the roof called to the others, asking if they'd felt anything.

"No," Jenna whispered, feeling in her bones a disaster was imminent.

The barn shuddered. There could be no doubt this time. The whole structure quivered like an animal twitching its skin. Men clung desperately to the timbers. The framework swayed one way, then the other.

Rob lost his grip. He dangled by one hand, swinging wildly with every movement of the barn. Wood shrieked and groaned as it was stressed beyond its limits.

"Hang on!" Jenna shrieked. "Rob, hang on!"

He couldn't have heard her in the din. But for a moment he looked straight at her, almost as if he'd read her mind.

Then she saw his hand slip from its hold.

And she watched him fall.

Chapter
10

"**R**ob!" Jenna cried. "Oh, no!"

She raced toward the swaying barn and heard the wooden timbers groan and snap. Men screamed as they clung to the shattering structure.

Then the whole framework collapsed. Timbers snapped in two like toothpicks. Splintered shards of wood flew in all directions as the barn crashed to the ground. A great cloud of dust puffed up, tossing stinging grains into the faces of the horrified watchers. The sharp smell of pine lanced the air.

Jenna's heart beat so hard she thought it would come right out of her chest. She could hear groans from beneath the wreckage. A man screamed, a sharp, tearing sound that scraped along her nerves until she thought she would scream with him.

She wasn't going to do Rob or anyone else any good if she panicked. Taking a deep breath, she steadied herself.

"Rob?" she called as she reached the wreckage. "Rob, can you hear me?"

He didn't answer.

Other people came to help. Jenna worked with the rescuers, pulling boards away to free the trapped men. There were a few broken bones and a lot of cuts and bruises, but it seemed they'd all been very lucky.

Jenna would have been relieved . . . if she'd found Rob. But she didn't see him anywhere.

"Please let him be all right," she murmured. "Please let him be all right."

She said it over and over, as if that might make it come true.

"Jenna!"

Recognizing Hallie's voice, Jenna turned. The other girl picked her way through the wreckage. Dirt smudged her face, and a long tear marred her skirt.

"You're all right?" Hallie demanded. She sounded almost like her old self, although a strange light glimmered in her glassy eyes.

Jenna nodded. "Are you?"

"I'm fine. Have you found Rob yet?"

"Not yet," Jenna replied. Somehow, she managed to keep her voice from shaking. "I think he's under there." She pointed toward the main section of wreckage.

"Oh, Jenna."

The girls looked at each other for a moment. Then they started working. Hallie never stopped and never complained. Jenna forgave her for the terrible things she'd said. Nothing else mattered except that she'd come to help when Jenna needed her most.

Then Jenna spotted a bit of cloth, buried beneath a mass of splintered wood. Pale-blue cloth, like Rob's shirt. She found a long plank that felt stable and crawled along it to get a better look.

Was he down there? Was he alive?

"Be careful!" Hallie called.

The plank shifted under her, and Jenna felt herself falling sideways, into the rubble. She clung to the wood and stood perfectly still. Her heart pounded wildly. Finally, she felt the beam settle into place. She began creeping along again.

Crawling as far as she dared, she peered into the wreckage. She saw a dark head of hair and the edge of a shirt.

Rob! His eyes were closed, and she couldn't see enough of his chest to tell if he still breathed. Or not. A thick heavy beam rested across his body, pinning him in place.

"Rob?" she called.

She stared at his face. He didn't move a muscle. His eyelids didn't even flicker. Then he opened his eyes and looked straight at her.

"Jenna!" he called in a strained voice. He coughed and squeezed his eyes shut again.

Her breath went out in a gasp of relief. "Are you all right? Can you move?"

"I think I'm all right," he groaned. "But I can't move. This beam is too heavy. My arms are trapped."

Jenna turned to Hallie. "Get help. Quickly!"

Jenna turned back to Rob. "It's going to be all right," she promised him. "Help is coming. Hang on."

"I'm trying, Jenna," Rob replied.

Jenna spotted several men running toward her. "Over here!" she shouted and waved. "Hurry!"

When the men reached her, they quickly cleared the

smaller pieces of wood away. Then they levered a timber beneath the heavy beam pinning Rob.

"When we lift the beam, young lady, you pull him out," one of the men said. "Can you do that?"

"Of course I can," Jenna told him.

He nodded. "All right, men. All together now."

Jenna heard them groan with effort as they bore down on the timber. The beam creaked and shuddered. Then it rose. An inch. Two. Up off Rob's chest. Rob gave a gasp of pain.

The beam rose higher. Grabbing Rob under the arms, Jenna tugged him out from under. The moment he was clear, she called to the other men. They eased the beam back down.

"Thanks," Rob muttered, holding one arm across his chest.

Jenna knelt beside him. "You're hurt!"

"I think it's just a few cracked ribs," he protested. His gaze went to the beam. "Right now, I'm feeling very lucky."

"You are lucky," one of the men told him. "Let's get you out of here so the doctor can look at you."

Rob nodded. Then he turned to Jenna and took her hand in both of his. "Thank you. I owe you for saving me, and I always pay my debts."

She blushed. "I didn't do anything, really."

"You did." He smiled. Then the smile vanished as he grimaced in pain.

"Go get yourself taken care of," she ordered.

Two of the men lifted him and carried him away. Jenna got to her feet and dusted her skirt off as best she could. As she did, she spotted something else beneath the pile of wood.

A hand.

"Look!" she cried, pointing.

The men leaped into action again. A whole section of framework had fallen in one piece and they had to lever it away. Finally, they reached the trapped man.

It was Frank Douglas. He lay on his back, his arms flung wide. His eyes stared blindly upward.

A two-by-four had pierced straight through his chest. Tattered flesh and bits of bone had sprayed up around the wood. A pool of blood surrounded Frank's body. Jenna stared, too horrified even to move. The blood spread, staining every board it touched.

She tried to look away, but couldn't. The pool grew larger still. She couldn't believe that a human body could hold so much blood. She saw the crimson pool creeping closer. In a moment, it will touch my shoes, she realized.

With a strangled cry, she leaped back. She covered her mouth with both hands.

"Oh," she gasped. "Oh, oh, oh!"

Someone laughed. Jenna instantly recognized that high-pitched giggle. Her skin crawled with horror as she turned to Hallie.

The other girl stood over Frank's body. Blood had soaked the hem of her skirt, staining it crimson. Tears streamed down her cheeks. Her blue eyes glimmered with a wild look.

She stood over the dead man, laughing.

She threw back her head and her golden hair came loose from its pins, streaming out over her shoulders.

"I wanted it to happen, and it did," she laughed.

"It did!"

Chapter
11

"Hallie!" Jenna cried. "What's wrong with you?"

Still Hallie laughed. She couldn't seem to stop. She fell to her knees and pressed her hands to her cheeks, laughing and laughing. A circle of onlookers stared at her as though she'd gone mad.

Jenna couldn't stand it any longer. She grabbed the other girl by the shoulders and shook her hard. Hallie gasped. Then the giggles turned to sobs. Tears ran down her face in a flood. They ran into her wide-open mouth. Hallie turned her face and pressed it into Jenna's skirt. Jenna held her head and stroked her hair.

"It's all right, Hallie. It's all right," she murmured. Jenna gazed around, feeling helpless. She didn't know what else to do.

Mr. Sheridan rushed up to them. "She's overwrought," he told Jenna. He swept Hallie into his arms and carried her away from the wreckage.

"Come, Jenna. We've got to get her home."

Hallie's mother joined them at the carriage and held Hallie in her arms during the ride home. Hallie soon stopped crying, but she stared straight ahead with a blank, haunted look that made Jenna feel uneasy.

As soon as they arrived at the house, Mrs. Sheridan led her daughter up to bed. Jenna followed. She watched Hallie fall deeply asleep the moment she stretched out across the bed.

"Is she going to be all right?" Jenna whispered.

Mrs. Sheridan turned to her. "Don't worry, dear. She'll be fine once she gets some sleep."

"Do you mind if I stay with her?" Jenna asked.

"That's a fine idea, Jenna. I know she'd love to find you here when she wakes," the older woman said.

She stroked her daughter's hair gently, then turned toward the door.

"Mrs. Sheridan?" Jenna called.

The older woman turned back. "Yes, Jenna?"

"Did you happen to see a . . . a shadow move over the barn before it fell?"

"A shadow?" Mrs. Sheridan repeated, frowning. "No. No one mentioned seeing a shadow. Jenna, dear . . . you're not feeling unwell, are you?"

"No, ma'am."

"Perhaps you should lie down—"

"I'm fine, really," Jenna insisted.

Mrs. Sheridan hesitated. Then she nodded. "All right. But if you should feel strange in any way, I want you to tell me right away."

"I'm fine," Jenna said again.

The older woman studied her. Then she smiled gently and turned away again. Jenna settled onto her own bed with a book. The room was silent except for Hallie's soft, regular breathing.

Jenna read the same paragraph several times, then set the book aside. She couldn't concentrate. An image of the terrible accident ran over and over again in her mind.

Hallie's voice echoed through her memory. *I wanted it to happen, and it did.*

And that shadow. Why hadn't anyone else seen it?

Jenna wasn't about to mention it again. Not after Mrs. Sheridan's reaction. People might start thinking she'd gone crazy. But she had seen it. And it had something to do with the barn falling, she felt certain.

Even more important, what was wrong with Hallie?

"Ohhhh," Hallie moaned softly.

Jenna got up to check on her. Hallie moaned again. Then she flung the covers aside and swung her legs over the side of the bed. She was about to get up, Jenna realized.

But her eyes remained closed.

"Hallie!" Jenna exclaimed, rushing to her friend.

The moment she touched Hallie, the other girl sank back into bed. Jenna heard her breathing slow down. Jenna watched her for a moment. Should she call Mrs. Sheridan? She decided not to. Maybe Hallie just had a bad dream. Perfectly natural under the circumstances.

"Let's get you back under the covers," Jenna muttered.

She lifted Hallie's legs back onto the bed and pulled

the light quilt up over her. As she tucked the edge of the cover around Hallie's shoulders, Jenna noticed a dark splotch on her friend's chest. Jenna leaned over and peered down at the mark.

She gasped. A horrible bruise marred the skin of Hallie's chest, right below the hollow of her throat. An ugly mark, so dark purple that it looked almost black. The gold locket gleamed against it.

Jenna's mind spun as she stared at the bruise.

Heart-shaped.

The exact size and shape of Hannah Fear's golden locket.

Chapter
12

Jenna chewed worriedly at her lip. She pushed the lace collar of Hallie's dress back and stared down at the disgusting bruise.

The necklace.

Almost as soon as she had put it on, Hallie had started acting strange. Could the necklace have some secret power? Had it taken control of Hallie somehow, forcing her to act so strangely?

"That's crazy," she muttered.

But was it?

And what about the crystal bracelet? Jenna wondered. What if I'd kept it on, the way Hallie wore the locket?

She went to the dresser and opened the top drawer. The iridescent crystal beads sparkled.

Julia's bracelet.

Jenna didn't want to touch it. She didn't want to

pick it up. But her hand stretched out, as if she had lost all control of her body. Her fingers plucked up the bracelet and gathered it in her palm.

The beads felt warm against her skin. Warm and pulsing, as if throbbing with a life all their own.

"You're imagining things," she muttered.

She glanced out the window. The sun shone brightly in the cloudless sky, and she thought she'd never seen a prettier day. That's what's real, she told herself. Not enchanted jewelry or haunted crypts.

The sight made her feel better. Calmer. Then she looked down at her hands. Her breath caught in her throat. Somehow, while she'd been gazing out the window, her hands had been busy.

Her own hands. They had undone the gold catch and had begun fitting the bracelet around her wrist.

Shuddering, she flung the bracelet away from her. It landed on the wooden floor with a tinkling sound. It glistened in the sunlight, tempting her to pick it up again.

She knew better.

"Now to rid you of your problem, Hallie," she whispered.

Taking a deep breath, she returned to the bed. The gold locket reflected the sunlight in a buttery gleam. As Jenna stared down at the locket, the light seemed to shift, piercing her eyes. She blinked, forced to look away.

Jenna didn't want to touch it. But she had to, for Hallie's sake.

She squinted into the blinding light and reached toward the locket. As her fingertips made contact, she gasped and pulled her hand away. Heat pulsed from the metal, singeing her fingertips.

Jenna set her teeth hard, reached out again and forced herself to ignore the burning feeling as she grasped the golden heart. She tugged on the locket to slide the catch around where she could reach it.

Finally, she grabbed the catch. But no matter how hard she tried, she couldn't undo it. It felt as though the clasp had fused into one piece. She tried to tug the necklace over Hallie's head. But the chain wasn't long enough. She had to break the chain, Jenna realized.

Winding it around her fingers, she began to pull. Harder and harder.

Hallie whimpered.

Jenna tightened her grip on the chain. Hallie moaned, a deep groan that made Jenna loosen her grip for a moment. Then Hallie thrashed her head from side to side. Jenna stared down at her friend as Hallie's face crumpled in a grimace of pain.

Impossible, Jenna thought. It shouldn't hurt. It couldn't hurt. And even if it did, she had to get this locket off of Hallie. Jenna believed her very life depended on it.

Jenna took a deep breath and gripped the chain tighter. She pulled as hard as she could.

Hallie's head remained still upon her pillow. Jenna watched her and saw two tears form at the corners of Hallie's eyes. But they looked strange. Dark. Red. The tears squeezed out of Hallie's eyes and flowed down her cheeks, dripping into the blond hair at her temples.

Staining it red.

With a gasp of horror, Jenna dropped the chain and stumbled backward. She stared down at Hallie. Her face had returned to normal. A small, peaceful smile curved her thin lips.

Jenna gazed at the two tiny patches of red marking her friend's hair. No, she had not imagined the whole thing.

Jenna felt her mouth go dry. Her knees trembled and she sat back on the edge of her bed, staring at Hallie.

She felt an impulse to call Hallie's mother. But she couldn't make a sound.

She took a deep breath. Mrs. Sheridan hadn't believed her when she'd mentioned the shadow. She wouldn't understand about this either.

Only one person in Shadyside might believe her story.

And try to help her.

Rob.

She had to find him.

Jenna slipped out the Sheridans' front door and dashed across the lawn before anyone noticed her leaving. Out on the road, she noticed thick gray clouds massing overhead.

Jenna walked quickly toward the Fear estate. A cool, moist breeze whipped stray tendrils of hair around her face. She could tell that it would rain soon.

"Just what I need," she muttered. Running part of the way, Jenna quickly came to the road where the Fears lived.

She walked as far as the drive that curved up to the

Fear mansion. She stopped, staring down that double strip of crushed rock. The gloomy mansion loomed up ahead at the top of the drive. It looked even darker and more ominous beneath the blanket of clouds.

She didn't want to see the Fears. Not now. Not ever again.

So she walked toward the back of the house, through the high grass at the edge of the estate. Rob had told her that he lived in the gardener's cottage. It had to be around here somewhere, Jenna assured herself.

She turned and looked back at the mansion. A single gabled window on the second story peered down at her like a Cyclops's eye. The window in Julia Fear's room, she thought.

She kept glancing at it over her shoulder, feeling that someone was watching her. Unease twitched along her nerves. Could someone be up in the window watching her? Jenna stood still for a second and peered up at it.

"Hello, Jenna."

Jenna froze. Her legs turned to water, nearly collapsing under her.

Slowly, she turned to face Angelica Fear.

Chapter

13

Dressed in a long, white gown and a trailing shawl, Angelica seemed to glow in the muted light. Jenna noticed leaves and twigs clinging to the hem of her dress and guessed that she'd been walking in the woods.

She carried a basket over her arm and Jenna spotted some spiky-looking plants inside.

"I gathered some wild mushrooms for dinner," Angelica murmured, shifting the basket to her other arm. "I'm so glad you came to visit, dear," she added with a smile.

"I, ah—"

"But why didn't you come straight up to the house? What are you doing wandering around back here?"

Jenna's heart thumped wildly. "I . . . I knocked on the door, but no one answered," she stammered. "I thought maybe you were out in the garden, so I—"

"And where's your sister?"

Jenna blinked. "Don't you mean my friend, Hallie?"

"Oh, yes. Of course." Laughing, Angelica waved her bejeweled hand. "Dear me, I think my memory is playing tricks on me these days. Of course, I mean your friend. Now, come in and join us for tea."

Jenna didn't move. She stood there, trying to think of an excuse not to go inside the Fears' awful mansion again. Angelica clasped her arm and turned her toward the house. Jenna felt her thin, cold fingers digging into her flesh. Jenna willed herself to remain still. But her feet moved forward, defying her will to resist.

One halting step.

And then another.

"That's my girl," Angelica murmured. "Only a few steps more. You seem a little tired, dear. Some tea and scones will refresh you," she promised.

As the house drew closer, Jenna felt her stomach twist into a knot. If she ever came out of there alive, she'd never, *ever* go near the place again.

"Do your hosts know you came to visit us?" Angelica asked.

"Oh, yes," Jenna lied. "They'll be expecting me home soon, so I can't stay long."

"That's a shame," Angelica murmured.

As they trudged up the stone staircase that led to the porch, Simon came out of the front door. His dark eyes glowed in his sharp-featured face. His thin lips twisted into a smile.

"Why, our pretty visitor has come again," he greeted Jenna.

He peered down at her. Jenna ducked her head, not wanting to meet his gaze.

"Her friend couldn't come," Angelica told him.

"Ah," he murmured. "Why not?"

"She's not feeling well," Jenna began to explain. "She got very upset today—"

"Not feeling well? Upset?" Angelica exclaimed. "What happened?"

Surprised, Jenna stared at her. "Didn't Rob tell you?"

"I didn't know you were acquainted with our Robert," Simon replied sharply.

Jenna felt like kicking herself. She never should have let them know that she knew Rob. She decided to make light of it.

"I met him this morning, at the barn raising," she told them. "He told me that he worked for you, so I assumed he'd tell you what happened."

"What barn raising?" Simon asked. Jenna heard a cold, hard edge in his words. "I thought Rob had been out in the woods all morning. Chopping firewood."

Jenna suddenly felt heartsick. She hadn't meant to get Rob in trouble with the Fears. What kind of hold did they have over him? He said he worked for them. Was he some sort of slave?

"Uh—the barn raising at the Millers," Jenna replied. "Maybe Rob forgot to tell you about it. There was an accident there. The barn came crashing down on top of the workers."

"How terrible," Simon sighed and shook his dark head.

"Simply awful," Angelica murmured. "Come have some tea and tell us all about it."

With her fingers still firmly wrapped around Jenna's forearm, Angelica led the way to the drawing room. The draperies remained closed again today and pockets of shadow clung to every corner.

The silver tea service and china dishes of cake stood on the wooden cart next to the sofa. Jenna knew she wouldn't be able to eat a thing.

She didn't think she'd *dare* eat anything.

"Sit right here next to me," Angelica softly ordered her. "I'll fix you a plate."

Jenna settled on the very edge of the sofa, as far from Angelica as she could manage. Simon sat down on the chair opposite her. His dark gaze settled on her and she felt as though he'd touched her with cold, clammy fingers.

"Why, Jenna, you're not wearing your bracelet," he observed. Jenna thought he sounded alarmed. She noticed Angelica's head pop up. Then she stared at Jenna's bare wrist.

Jenna held herself very still. "Uh . . . no."

"Don't you like it?" Simon asked.

"I do like it," Jenna protested. "It's lovely. Really."

Angelica handed Jenna a cup of tea. Jenna felt her hand tremble as she grasped the saucer. She heard the teacup rattle loudly and she quickly rested the cup and saucer on her knee. She gazed over at Angelica to see if she had noticed.

Angelica's green eyes glittered with a cold, hard edge.

"My feelings might be hurt if I thought you didn't like Julia's bracelet," she confided to Jenna in a soft voice.

"I didn't mean to hurt your feelings," Jenna replied. "The bracelet felt very loose. I was afraid of losing it," she lied.

Angelica and Simon exchanged a look. Smoldering brown eyes stared into green ones, and Jenna got the creepy feeling that they'd passed some sort of message to each other.

"Don't you want to hear about the accident?" Jenna asked, desperate to change the subject.

Angelica's gaze snapped back to her. "By all means, dear," she answered.

Jenna quickly described the terrible accident. She almost found herself describing the dark cloud that she'd seen moving over the barn just before it started to fall. Then she caught herself. She wasn't quite sure why. But she didn't want the Fears to know she'd noticed the strange, ominous shadow.

Angelica and Simon stared at her intently as she spoke. "Was anyone killed?" Angelica asked quietly.

Jenna felt chilled by her question. It wasn't the words, but the look on Angelica's face when she asked it. Almost as if she relished the thought of someone dying. Simon leaned closer to hear her answer. Jenna noticed the same look of suppressed excitement on his face.

"One person died," Jenna reluctantly told them.

"How exactly?" Simon inquired.

Jenna's stomach twisted and churned. "W-what do you mean?"

"Well, you've described the scene so vividly for us up until now, dear," Angelica cut in. "Tell us a little more about this poor, unfortunate soul. Was it a fall? A broken neck, perhaps?"

"No, it wasn't his neck," Jenna shook her head.

"Uh, he . . . he . . ." She closed her eyes to shut out the sight of the two people staring so avidly at her. "I don't want to talk about it anymore, if you don't mind."

"Look at me, Jenna," Simon ordered.

His voice was soft, even friendly. But it pierced Jenna like a frigid blast of winter wind. Opening her eyes, she looked straight into Simon's depthless black pupils. She felt trapped.

"Now, tell us," he asked again. "How did the man die?"

Jenna fought to refuse. But it seemed as though her voice had taken on a life of its own. And it wanted to obey Simon Fear.

"A board went through him," she whispered.

"Where?" Angelica asked.

"It . . . it went through his chest."

"There must have been a great deal of blood," Angelica murmured.

Jenna felt sick, remembering how that red pool had crept toward her. Yes. A great deal of blood. Her hand shook, and her spoon rattled loudly against the saucer.

Simon gazed at his wife. Their expressions didn't change, but Jenna could feel a change in the air. Tension filled the room, a nerve-tingling sense of anticipation.

Maybe it's the storm approaching, she thought.

Then again, maybe not.

You've got to get out of here, Jenna urged herself. You've got to see Rob and tell him about Hallie. Jenna set her cup aside and pushed up from the sofa.

"You can't go yet," Simon objected sharply.

One part of her wanted to obey, to sit back down and await whatever he had in mind. But then she thought about Hallie. She had to save Hallie.

She didn't know where the strength came from, but she forced herself to remain standing. She made herself look at him.

"I'm sorry," she said politely. "I told the Sheridans I'd be back in an hour, and I'm late now. I have to go. I don't want them to worry."

Simon's eyes narrowed. Before he could say anything, however, Angelica cleared her throat.

"Simon, dear, we shouldn't keep our pretty young guest a moment longer," she said.

"You're right," he said, rising. "I'm sorry we couldn't talk longer, Jenna," he added, gazing grimly down at her. "We'll spend more time together on your next visit. I promise you," he added solemnly.

A lump of sheer terror rose in Jenna's throat. She didn't intend to return here. Ever. But Simon Fear sounded so sure.

As if he could *make* her come no matter what she wanted.

She hurriedly thanked them for tea, then started to leave. To her relief, Simon didn't accompany her. Angelica followed her, chatting on about the weather as they walked to the door.

"It was so good to see you again, Jenna," Angelica cooed, holding the front door open for her guest. "Next time, be sure to bring your friend Hallie with you."

Jenna scurried down the stone steps as quickly as she could without running. If Angelica hadn't been watching, she would have raced pell-mell for the road.

"Come again soon, Julia!" Angelica called.

That brought Jenna to a stop. Slowly, she turned toward Angelica. She suddenly felt cold, as if someone had replaced her blood with ice water.

"You mean Jenna, don't you, Mrs. Fear?" she asked.

"That's what I said, dear," Angelica replied.

Jenna studied her for a moment. Then she turned and started walking again. Faster this time. She couldn't wait to get away from here. Angelica might have *thought* she'd said Jenna. But she hadn't. She'd said Julia.

She'd mistaken Jenna for Julia Fear.

Her dead daughter.

Chapter
14

Jenna's mind raced wildly. Angelica had called her Julia.

No reason to panic, she calmed herself. Maybe the Fears are just strange. Maybe their minds have been twisted by grief after losing their daughters.

But that didn't explain the necklace.

And it didn't explain the bracelet.

Or poor Hallie.

Jenna strode quickly down the Fears' long drive. Tears blurred her vision. She dashed them away with the back of her hand. She couldn't fall apart now. She wouldn't let herself.

But what should she do? If she tried to confide in the Sheridans, they'd probably pack her up and send her home on the next train out of Shadyside.

She'd be safe from the Fears.

But what about Hallie?

What about Rob?

She had to speak with Rob. Even if he couldn't help her, she could at least warn him about the Fears.

Angry-looking clouds filled the sky, making it look nearly as dark as nightfall. Jenna heard thunder off in the distance. She lifted her skirt and ran along the edge of the woods.

The first drops of rain splashed loudly among the leaves. Jenna felt the rain on her face and hair. Soaking through her clothes.

A bolt of lightning stabbed across the sky. Jenna flinched. She'd never liked storms. The wind tossed the branches, and the rain started falling so hard she could only see a few feet ahead of her. Her feet splashed into a puddle so deep that water poured in the tops of her ankle-high boots.

"Oh, no," she muttered, shaking first one foot, then the other.

Lightning flared again. In the brief, searing glare, she spotted a dark, blocky shape just ahead. A building!

"Please let it be Rob's cottage," she said aloud.

Lifting her skirts with both hands, she scurried through the wet grass. As she neared the structure, she saw that it was more a hut than a cottage. A huge old oak tree shaded it.

"Rob?" she called, knocking at the door. "Rob, are you in there? It's Jenna."

The door swung open. Inside, the single room was shrouded in shadows. She could see the shape of a table and the pale rectangles of curtained windows.

A foul odor wrapped around her. She covered her mouth and nose with her hand. Ugh, how awful! she thought. A horrid, rotten smell filled her nose and she covered her face with her hands.

"Got to have some light," she gasped with her hands pressed over her nose and mouth.

She stepped forward, toward the barely seen shape of the table in the center of the room. She groped along the tabletop, searching for a lamp or candle. Feeling the smooth column of a candlestick, she pulled it toward her. Again by touch, she found a box of matches.

She struck a match and lit the candle. The flickering light spread as the flame leaped and sputtered.

Jenna looked up.

Then she screamed.

A face hovered in the shadow-shrouded corner of the room.

Jenna gasped and jumped backward. With a shock, she realized the horrible, staring thing wasn't a face at all.

It was a skull. A human skull.

Jenna suddenly felt faint. The room began to spin and her sight grew blurry. She felt her legs give way under her and she grabbed the back of a chair.

She had to get out of here. She pressed her hand to her forehead.

Jenna took a breath, gagging on the rank, putrid-smelling air. She lifted her head and looked up.

The skull stared back at her through vacant eyes.

Long, white teeth glistened in its fleshless jaw. Moving slowly, numbly, like a person in a dream, Jenna lifted the candle from the table and stumbled toward the door.

The flickering circle of light spread, bringing more

of the room into sight. Shelves lined the walls, and every shelf held bones. Arm bones and leg bones, skeletal hands lying stark and white against the wood.

She turned in one direction, then another. The candle spat wax onto her hand, but she didn't notice. She didn't feel anything but fear.

Bones. Bones. Bones everywhere.

The story! The story Hallie had told in the grave-yard that first night. Julia and Hannah Fear, their bodies buried without bones. Their skeletons walking . . .

"No!" Jenna gasped.

Whirling, she ran from the cabin. The candle sput-tered and died in the rain. She flung it from her. All she wanted was to get away from that horrible place. Because now there could be no doubts, no sensible explanations. Now, she knew the truth.

The Fears were evil.

Pure evil.

She had to get to Rob. For his help, yes. But also to warn him. He might be in danger, too.

She dashed along the line of trees. Rain pelted into her face. *Please let me find him,* she thought franti-cally. *Please!*

Finally, she caught sight of a faint glow in the trees ahead. A light!

The flickering yellow glow gave her the strength to stagger forward. Gasping with effort, she stumbled toward it. Soon she spotted another building tucked beneath the rain-heavy branches of the trees. The yellow glow spilled from the single window.

She approached slowly, ready to run at any mo-ment. Holding her breath, she peeked in the window.

Then she saw Rob. He sat up in bed, his back propped up against a nest of pillows. A white bandage was wrapped around his chest. His face looked a little pale and drawn, but other than that, he seemed fine.

"At last," she breathed.

She rushed around to the front door. Finding it locked, she rapped sharply with her fist.

"Who is it?" Rob called.

"Jenna," she replied. "Hurry, Rob. Let me in!"

It felt like forever before he opened the door. The moment it swung open, she rushed inside. Slamming the door behind her, she quickly latched it. "Close the curtain," she ordered.

"What's the matter, Jenna?" he asked.

"Please, just do as I say."

He did what she asked. Now that she was safe, she started to shake. To her embarrassment, her teeth started to chatter. The noise seemed loud in the quiet room.

"Come sit down," he ordered, leading her over to the table.

She sat heavily in the chair he pulled out for her. Her legs felt rubbery and sore. Rob brought her a cup of water. She held the cup with both hands and sipped gratefully. After a few minutes, she felt her breathing and pounding heart slow down.

"What's the matter?" he asked.

"It's going to sound incredible," she burst out. "But I swear every word is true."

She told him the story about the Fear girls' deaths. She told him about Hannah Fear's necklace and the way Hallie had been acting since she started wearing it. She told him about the bruise, and the ominous shadow that had enveloped the barn.

"There's a cabin right here on the estate," she continued breathlessly. "And it's full of bones."

"Bones?" He frowned. "But I've been in every building on this estate, and I've never seen any bones."

Jenna took a deep, shuddering breath. "I'm scared. I'm more scared than I've ever been in my life."

"You saved my life today. Do you think I'm going to let anything bad happen to you?"

"But—"

"I promise," he told her. "I will protect you. Jenna, if the Fears are truly evil, then they have to be stopped. First thing in the morning, I'll look around. The Fears hardly notice I'm around anymore. I'll find out what's going on," he assured her. "Everything will be . . ."

His voice trailed off. For a moment, his eyes went completely blank. Frighteningly blank. Rob's eyes closed and his face went pale.

"Rob? Are you all right?" Jenna asked him. Maybe he'd been hurt worse then he'd told her.

Then he blinked. He opened his eyes and his color seemed to return. He looked like the same Rob she'd come to know.

Still, something cold and frightened lurked in her mind. And she'd never felt so alone.

". . . As good as new," he finished, as if there hadn't been any break at all.

Jenna got to her feet. "I have to go home now," she told him. "The Sheridans will be frantic with worry."

He started to get up with her. Then his face twisted with pain, and he sank back into his chair. Weariness clouded his eyes. "You can find your way home all right?"

"Of course," she assured him.

She left the cottage, closing the door behind her. Her mind spun with questions as she made her way into the woods.

Wind gusted through the branches overhead. And then she heard the sound that had haunted the edges of her dreams. The sound she'd once thought a figment of her imagination, the sound she dreaded more than anything in the world.

The sound of wings.

Jenna looked up, terrified at what she might see.

Chapter
15

Jenna shrank back against the nearest tree trunk. She squinted into the darkness. She felt the rain on her face and heard her own ragged breathing.

And then, something else. The wings. Beating. Beating. Beating. Coming closer with each beat of her pounding heart.

Not an owl this time.

The trees loomed threateningly overhead. Even the dripping sky seemed to hang lower. Mist curled up from the ground, touching her skin with its clammy touch.

And still the wings came. Closer. Closer.

"No," she gasped. "No!"

Hurling herself forward, she raced headlong through the trees. Every crashing step shook her to her bones. Every breath felt like fire in her lungs. Still, she heard the sound up above. Somewhere in the dark sky. Swooping toward her. Right overhead.

Jenna ran on and on, not daring to glance up or even over her shoulder. Her wet skirts clung to her legs, their weight dragging at her. Sobbing with terror, she struggled forward. She had no idea which way she was going. Away. That was the important thing.

Spotting a light ahead, she turned in that direction. Maybe she'd come to a house. Maybe she had run right to the Sheridans' without realizing it.

Wings flapped above her head.

With a strangled cry, she flung herself forward. She crashed through the bushes and rolled out into a clearing. It had her now. Jenna squeezed her eyes closed. She sensed an immense dark shadow moving her. She heard the beating sound of huge wings.

So close now, she could feel the air stirred by their motion.

She curled her body into a small, tight ball of terror as she prepared herself for the worst.

Then the sound stopped.

Jenna lay still for a moment. She took a deep breath. She suddenly realized she remained unharmed.

Untouched.

But it had been right on her! It could have gotten her at any time. Had it simply flown past? Slowly, hesitantly, she opened her eyes.

And then she knew why she'd been spared.

She didn't lie in a clearing. She hadn't reached the Sheridans' house. Or any other.

She'd ended up in the cemetery.

In front of the Fear crypt.

She hadn't run to safety. She'd run straight into

danger. No, she thought as despair chilled her heart, she'd been *led* there.

The seconds ticked by with incredible slowness. Finally, she dared to move. Slowly, hesitantly, she rose to her feet.

She glanced over her shoulder at the cemetery gate. Maybe she could make it before . . .

Creak!

Her heart clenched. That noise! It sounded like stone grinding against stone. Terror swept over her, darker and stronger than anything she'd ever felt before. She shrank back against the nearest tree. Pressing her cheek against the rough, wet bark.

Creak!

She tried not to look at the stone angel perched above the crypt. But her gaze felt irresistibly drawn to it.

Droplets hung from the stone angel's wings. Each one shone like a blue-white diamond in the unearthly glow.

Jenna pressed closer to the sheltering trunk. Then she felt a change in the bark beneath her hand. It was more than wet. It was *slimy*. Pulling away, she started to wipe her hands. That was when she saw the red stain all over her palms. Then, right before her horrified gaze, more slick, warm liquid oozed out from the cracks in the bark.

She glanced down, and saw a hundred tiny red stains on her gown. Automatically, she looked up. More drops fell. They ran into her mouth, and tasted coppery and awful.

She scrubbed her mouth with her sleeve. Then a realization hit her.

The trees were bleeding!

Chapter
16

Jenna reeled away from the tree. Blood spattered her gown, her face, her arms. She wanted to scream. Instead, she pressed both hands over her mouth.

If she made a sound, someone . . . some*thing* might hear.

The air felt charged, as if lightning might strike at any moment.

But lightning could never charge the air with this eerie energy. Jenna knew it instinctively.

Something more gathered here. Something wicked and vile.

She could feel it watching her. Watching. And waiting. Its evil vibrations pulsed in the air.

Every moment, it grew stronger.

She tried to run, but her legs felt wooden. Lifeless. She couldn't move.

She noticed a faint movement on the front wall of

the mausoleum. A crack. Even as her mind tried to make sense of that, the crack widened.

No, not widened, she realized. Darkened.

Something thick and red welled up from the crack. More cracks appeared. Drops became rivulets, which joined to become streams. Soon the walls were running wet with blood.

Blood. Blood dripping from the trees, blood running from the crypt to form a glistening black pool just in front of the door. The stone angel's reflection shimmered in its depths.

Whirling, Jenna raced for the gate. She dodged through the headstones, slipping, sliding, clutching at anything she could to keep her balance.

Behind her, something rustled.

She cast a glance over her shoulder. The mist had risen higher, almost obscuring the headstones. Below it, running along the ground, was another kind of mist.

A black mist. Shadows.

They were coming after her. She could see dark tendrils coiling along the ground, swallowing her footprints.

A branch snagged her skirt and she stumbled. She hit the hard ground face first.

"No," she gasped. "Please, no!"

She scrambled onto her hands and knees. With a quick glance she saw the black mist closing in on her. It came boiling over the top of a headstone just a few yards away. The putrid smell of rot and waste washed over her. She gagged and coughed, forcing herself to crawl forward. Inch by inch.

A few moments more, and it would reach her. Cover her. Consume her.

Jenna staggered to her feet. But the moment she tried to take a step, she found herself still caught by the branch. Bending, she groped to free herself.

But her fingertips didn't feel a tree branch clinging to her skirt. She touched something cold and very smooth. Jenna felt the hair rise up on the nape of her neck.

She tugged at her skirt and finally looked down.

And saw the bony, white skeleton hand that held her in its grasp.

Chapter
17

Sobbing in terror, Jenna yanked hard on her skirt. Up ahead, she could see the black mist quickly oozing toward her.

Terror surged through her. With a gasp, she tore loose from the bony fingers and hurled herself backward.

Panting and clawing at the soft dirt, Jenna scrambled away on hands and knees. Then, leaping to her feet, she raced toward the cemetery gate. She didn't know why, but she felt sure that if she could just get past that entrance, she would be safe.

The cemetery gate loomed up eerily in the fog. Moisture glistened on the iron curlicues and dripped from the arch. Jenna hurled herself toward it. Out of the corner of her eye, she saw a single thick tendril of black mist snake toward her.

To drag her back.

With a desperate lunge, she flung herself at the gate. The doors crashed open. She hurtled through, landing hard on the road beyond. Gasping, she leaped up and slammed the gate closed.

Just in time, she thought, as the squirming blackness reached the gate. Almost overwhelmed by the awful stench of it, she staggered backward.

The shadows oozed and squirmed against the gate. But they didn't come past it. Some invisible barrier kept them imprisoned in the graveyard.

"I made it!" she gasped, hardly believing her luck.

Whirling around, she headed toward home.

She had to help Hallie.

It started to rain again, a steady downpour that soaked Jenna to the skin. Lightning slashed across the clouds. She hurried toward the back of the Sheridans' house, anxious to get inside before the next thunderstorm hit.

But even in the midst of the storm, everything looked so peaceful here. Normal. It seemed impossible to Jenna that horror thrived so near.

"Nothing seems to be impossible in Shadyside," she muttered under her breath.

She started to open the door. What would she tell the Sheridans? she wondered. They must be frantic, wondering where she'd disappeared to.

As she hesitated in the doorway, she caught sight of a pale figure, flitting through the trees behind the house. Her heart stopped.

For a moment, she expected to see the stone angel come flapping out of the woods, all fangs and claws and staring, empty eyes.

Lightning flashed, and Jenna glimpsed a mass of blond curls around the figure's head.

Hallie.

Clad only in her nightgown, she stumbled around the yard in the storm.

Jenna ran toward her. "Hallie!" she called.

Maybe she's walking in her sleep, Jenna thought. But an even worse thought lanced through her mind: Or maybe the Fears are calling her.

The other girl flashed a glance over her shoulder. Then she started to run. Dressed in only the long white gown, Jenna thought she looked like a ghost flitting through the trees.

"Hallie!" Jenna cried again. "Wait for me!"

The rain pelted down hard now, almost blinding Jenna. She pushed herself to keep up with Hallie's swiftly moving shape. Sick with horror, she realized where Hallie was going.

The cemetery.

"No, Hallie!" she shouted. "You can't go there. Stop! Listen to me. *Hallieeee!*"

The wind caught Jenna's words and tossed them back at her. Hallie swiftly flew ahead of her, as though she'd become part of the storm.

Jenna heard a huge bolt of lightning crackle overhead and in the sudden flash of light, she caught a glimpse of the cemetery gates. The misty shadows were gone. But Jenna knew they still waited. Watched and waited, there in the graveyard.

For Hallie, and for her.

"No!" she cried.

Hallie reached the gate. Grasping the latch, she started to open it. Jenna pushed herself to catch up.

She hurled her body against the gate, slamming it closed again.

The other girl spun toward her. Jenna saw no spark of recognition in Hallie's blank eyes. And not a single spark of emotion.

Jenna faced her. "Hallie," she panted. "Can you hear me?"

Hallie stared at Jenna, her blue eyes huge and glassy.

"Hallie?" Jenna whispered. Jenna saw her blink. Had she heard her? Was she coming back to her senses?

Then Hallie swiftly raised her arms and lunged at her. Sinking one hand deep into Jenna's hair, she dragged her back to the gate. Jenna fought desperately, kicking and struggling.

But Hallie's strength overpowered her. Hallie was too strong.

She dragged Jenna to the gates and then through.

Jenna screamed and called out her friend's name.

Hallie never made a sound or changed expression. It was unreal. Horrible. Worse than anything that had gone before, because this was her *friend*. Jenna felt as if she'd stepped into a nightmare.

Steadily, relentlessly, Hallie dragged her toward the mausoleum. The blood had disappeared, but the crypt still glowed with that ugly, unearthly light.

With a cry, Jenna tore free. But she was off balance, and couldn't stop herself from falling. She landed flat on her back. Stunned, she gasped for breath. Hallie bent and hauled her to her feet.

"Leave me alone!" Jenna screamed. She grabbed Hallie's nightgown and shoved her away.

Hallie's nightgown tore. Jenna's mind went numb when she saw what had happened to her friend.

No, her mind shrieked, frozen with disbelief. *No, no, no, nonononononono!*

The locket had sunk right into Hallie's chest . . . and the skin had grown over it.

Beneath the thin covering of skin, the gold heart pulsed with an unearthly light all its own.

Chapter
18

———

With an odd, jerky movement, Hallie turned and stared at Jenna with vacant blue eyes.

"Hallie, it's me, Jenna," she shouted desperately, running backward from her friend. If only she could break Hallie's awful trance. "You know me. I'm your best friend."

Hallie's eyes remained vacant. Blank. Cold and lifeless.

"Hallie, please listen to me. Don't you remember your mother and father? Don't you remember anyone?"

Hallie might have been a wooden doll. No, Jenna thought, her skin crawling with horror, a puppet. Arms and legs controlled by some other power.

Jenna felt desperate. "Do you remember our Sister Oath? We were six. We'd climbed into that big maple tree in my backyard, as high up as we could get. We swore to always protect each other, to watch out for each other. Please remember. Please!"

For a moment, she thought a flicker of light shone in Hallie's eyes.

But that flicker soon died. And Jenna's last hope with it.

Hallie slid forward, moving with an eerie, unnatural grace. The breeze lashed her wet hair into wild tendrils around her face and neck.

And beneath her skin, the locket beat like a second heart.

Jenna backed away. If Hallie caught her again, they would both be lost. If she ever hoped to save Hallie, she had to get away now.

With terrifying quickness, Hallie lunged at her. Jenna lost her balance. Hallie sat on Jenna's stomach, grabbing her by the throat.

Jenna couldn't breathe. She needed air! She clawed frantically at Hallie's hands.

But Hallie didn't let up. She kept squeezing and squeezing, and there was nothing Jenna could do to stop her. A huge bolt of lightning cracked open the sky. The searing illumination cast a silver halo around Hallie's pale hair.

Black spots swam across Jenna's vision. She felt her lungs about to burst.

I'm going to die, Jenna thought.

Here. Now.

"Enough."

A voice rolled like thunder out of the night.

Simon Fear.

Instantly, Hallie released her. She leaped to her feet and stood still.

Coughing, Jenna rolled onto her side.

"Hello, Jenna," Simon called.

It took every bit of Jenna's courage to get to her feet and turn toward that voice.

The Fears. Simon and Angelica.

They stood in front of the mausoleum, smiling.

Angelica wore the same white dress and shawl Jenna had seen her in that afternoon. She looks like an angel, Jenna thought.

Beside her, Simon stood tall and straight. His long, thin face looked even more haggard and sharper-edged. His lips curled in a grin that was more like a snarl. Light glinted off his teeth. To Jenna, he looked like an animal that had learned to walk like a man.

At that moment, Jenna would have thrown herself off a cliff to escape them. But she could only stand, watching. And waiting.

She wanted so badly to run. But felt frozen with terror.

"You won't get away with this!" Jenna cried.

Angelica's smile widened. Her eyes glittered like green stones. "But, my dear, we already have."

Shadows came oozing out of the open door of the mausoleum. Thick, black tendrils coiled around the Fears. Swirling. Stroking. They seemed to blend with Angelica's raven hair—and Simon's night-dark eyes. Something lurked just inside the doorway of the crypt. Something that watched. Something that waited. Something . . .

"You belong to us." Simon's voice was only a whisper, but it shook her right down to her soul. "Julia."

"I'm Jenna!" she cried. "Jenna!"

Simon flung his head back and laughed.

Jenna stepped back and stared at the statue.

The heavy wings shivered. Then lifted.

It opened its eyes and stared straight at Jenna.

"No!" Jenna gasped. She stumbled backward, throwing up her arm to ward off that terrible, inhuman stare.

CRACK! The angel pulled one arm free, then another. Then it straightened. Now, Jenna could see that its legs bent backward, like an insect's.

Wings flapped above Jenna's head and she cried out in despair. A gust of air knocked her to her knees. The angel hovered over her, its neck scaly and curved like a snake's.

She felt a chill as a cold, dark shadow swept over her.

Jenna dared to look up. The angel smiled. Angelica's smile. With horrible swiftness, it dropped toward her.

The dark wings enclosed her, surrounded her.

Smothered her.

The blackness swallowed her.

Chapter
19

Light seeped through Jenna's closed lids. She opened her eyes and saw a dank, windowless room. Chunks of mold and thick gray cobwebs clung to the stone walls and ceiling. The rough stone floor under her felt gritty and damp. A single lantern hung from a hook on the far wall. Its meager light left pockets of shadows in the corners.

This has to be the Fears' mansion, she thought. Down in the basement. A band of icy-cold dread squeezed her heart.

Slowly, she pushed herself to a sitting position. She reached up with shaking hands to massage her brow.

The soft sound of breathing made her turn. Hallie stood a few feet away, her expression blank. Her hair had dried into filthy clumps, and her muddy night-gown clung to her, stained and torn. She hardly looked human.

"Hallie," Jenna whispered.

But the other girl remained as stiff and still as a block of wood. Her skin looked waxy, as though all the blood had been drained out of it. Jenna knew then that her friend had slipped still deeper under the Fears' evil spell.

Still, she had to try.

"You have to wake up, Hallie," she begged. "Please, I know you can hear me. Please try!"

Hallie didn't even blink. Beneath the skin of her chest, the locket glowed. Hesitantly, Jenna reached for the chain. Was there some way to get it off her?

Hallie reacted swiftly. Her eyes narrowed, and her lips drew back in an animal's snarl. She raised clawed hands to ward Jenna off.

"There has to be a way," she muttered.

If there was, she couldn't find it. Tears stung her eyes, tears she had no way of stopping. She was completely, totally alone. Even if the Sheridans tried to look for her, they'd never find her here.

Not in time anyway.

The Fears had plenty of time to carry out their awful plans.

She sat down beside Hallie. Drawing her knees up, she wrapped her arms around them. The other girl stood like a statue, not moving, hardly even breathing.

"I wish you were here," Jenna murmured, glancing up at her. "Really here. I want my best friend back. We could fight them then!"

Hallie made no answer. Jenna rested her forehead on her knees and tried not to think.

The door rattled. Startled, she jerked her head up. Someone was coming!

Swiftly, she stretched out on her side, pretending to be unconscious. She watched the door from beneath the shelter of her arm. Something moved in the darkness beyond the window.

Her breath stopped as she heard the scrape of metal on metal. She saw the latch quiver, then begin to turn.

The door opened. But instead of Angelica and Simon, Rob stepped onto the first step.

"Rob!" she gasped.

He held one finger to his lips. Then he reached back through the doorway and grabbed a shovel. Closing the door softly behind him, he ran down the stairs. Jenna sat up. He knelt beside her, but kept his gaze on the door.

"What are you doing here?" she whispered. "How did you find us?"

"I sneaked in the house to look around," he told her, his voice as quiet as hers. "I saw them bring you in. But I couldn't get past the Fears for a while. Finally, they went out, and I came for you."

"You've put yourself in terrible danger—" she began.

"I told you once that I wouldn't let anything happen to you," he said. "Did you think I didn't mean it?"

He took her by the hand and drew her to her feet. "Come on. We've got to get out of here."

"Wait!" she hissed, tugging on him. "We can't go without Hallie."

Rob's expression turned grim. "We can't do anything for her, Jenna. She's lost."

"No!" Jenna insisted. "We have to take her."

"Jenna, you don't understand what's going on here."

She started to shake her head, but he grabbed her by the shoulders. "While I was hiding in the house, I heard Simon and Angelica talking. For years, he and Angelica have been trying to find a way to bring their daughters back to life."

"What?" Jenna gasped.

"And now they've found a way."

Jenna felt too afraid to ask. But she had to. "How, Rob? How do they plan to do it?"

"It takes another life. Another spirit. They take a living person's spirit and put it in a dead person. And the corpse lives and breathes. That's why they brought you and Hallie here."

Jenna shook her head. Rejecting the absolute horror of what he'd said. They wanted her spirit. And Hallie's.

"Even the names," she moaned. "Jenna . . . Julia. Hallie . . . Hannah. And the Fears were so pleased that Hallie and I were as close as sisters."

"That's right," Rob agreed. "Now, let's go. Hallie is already lost in the evil. You can't—"

He broke off abruptly, his head turning with a jerk. "Shh. I think someone is coming."

Jenna covered her mouth with her hands. She was so scared that she was afraid she might start screaming uncontrollably.

As if he knew what she was thinking, Rob turned back. Gently, he laid his hand on her shoulder. It was only for a moment, but that brief touch steadied her.

Grabbing the shovel, he crouched in the shadows at the bottom of the stairs.

The door opened with a creak that shredded Jenna's nerves. Simon Fear entered, carrying a large trunk. She guessed it was heavy by the way he grunted as he hauled it down the stairs.

She didn't want to know what was inside.

She saw a slight movement in the shadows where Rob had hidden. Jenna swallowed hard. This was their chance, their one chance.

Simon groaned with effort, and it seemed to take him forever to maneuver down the stairs. Once, he nearly dropped the trunk. But he caught it and heaved it into a more secure position in his arms.

Jenna felt ready to scream by the time he reached the bottom. Under her breath, she prayed that Angelica wasn't following.

Simon stared over at Jenna, and she shivered.

"Why are you doing this?" she demanded.

He smiled at her. "I think you already know."

"It won't work," she told him, barely keeping her voice from shaking. "It's unnatural. It *can't* work."

With a laugh, he flung his head back. "Oh, poor, misguided Jenna. Don't you know that the unnatural works all the time . . . when the *Fears* command it to?"

"You're evil!" she cried.

"Why, yes," he agreed. "We are."

Rob slipped out of hiding. Sneaking up behind Simon, he raised the shovel high. Jenna held her breath. *Please let it work. Please let us get away!* And then, with all his strength, Rob swung the shovel down.

Straight at Simon Fear's head.

Chapter
20

Simon whirled to face Rob. "Stop," he commanded.

The shovel halted a few inches from Simon's head. Rob's eyes grew wide in astonishment. He set his jaw and tried again. Jenna saw his muscles quiver as he struggled to make them obey.

But some power had taken over his body and he couldn't move.

Jenna clenched her fists. "Leave him alone!" she cried.

Carefully, Simon set the trunk down on the floor. Then he turned to her, his lips stretched in a terrible smile. "Isn't this sweet?" he drawled. "The hero comes to the rescue. But it turns out he isn't much of a hero after all."

He swung back around to face Rob. "Drop the shovel."

Rob's hand opened. The clatter of the shovel hitting the floor sent echoes bouncing around the room.

Simon reached into his pocket and drew out a small object. It caught the light and sent it back in a shower of blue-white sparks. Jenna gasped. The crystal bracelet! Somehow he had retrieved it from her room.

"Now," Simon ordered. "Put it on Jenna's arm."

Rob tried to resist. But his arm lifted, and he took the bracelet from Simon. Then Rob turned toward Jenna.

She gasped as Rob grabbed her arm and fastened the bracelet around her wrist. Instantly, her skin began to tingle. But nothing more happened.

"Now go back where you were," Simon told Rob.

Rob obeyed. Despair dulled his eyes as he looked at the man who forced his own body to work against him. "What have you done to me?" he rasped.

"We gave you life," Angelica announced.

With a shocked gasp, Jenna looked up at the doorway. Angelica stood at the top of the stairs. Her hair hung around her shoulders like a black cloak. The white streak stood out starkly.

Behind her, shadows lurked in the doorway. They coiled about her, blending with her black hair. Her face seemed to float in blackness.

"What did you say?" Rob demanded.

She started downstairs, walking gracefully, her hand on the iron railing. Smiling. She stopped in front of Rob. Running one pointed fingernail down his cheek, she looked into his eyes.

"I said we gave you life," she told him.

"No," Rob whispered.

Angelica laughed softly. "Do you remember where you came from?"

He shook his head. A terrible look flashed in his eyes. More than fear. More than despair. Jenna took a step toward him. But Simon turned his black gaze on her, and terror froze her where she stood.

"Now, Robert," Angelica continued. "There have been times when you tried to remember your past, and couldn't."

"I blacked out," he admitted.

"That is because you were dead," she told him.

"No," he whispered, his eyes wide with horror.

"Yes," Simon countered. His smile was cruel, and so were his eyes. "You were an experiment. If we could bring you back to life, and keep you alive, then we'd perfected a way to bring our daughters back."

Jenna began to tremble. Her heart beat so fast and hard that she was sure everyone else could hear it. "You killed him," she accused.

Angelica looked at her. Jenna had never seen such malice on a human face, and the sight chilled her to her soul.

"Of course we killed him," Angelica said.

Rob looked as stunned as Jenna felt. "It . . . it can't be true."

"Of course it's true." Simon's smile faded. "But you've disobeyed us, Rob. You worked against us. That wasn't in our plan. That is a problem I didn't foresee. But that problem will soon be at an end."

Rob frowned, obviously not understanding. But Jenna did.

"What do you mean?" he asked.

"It means . . ." Simon paused, and Jenna knew it was on purpose. He liked tormenting people. "It means that at the time we reanimated you, we hadn't yet figured out how to make the process permanent."

Jenna closed her eyes. This was too terrible to be real. She had to be dreaming. But when she opened her eyes again, she was still a prisoner.

"No," Rob gasped. "No."

"Yes," Simon corrected. "You were most useful, Rob. You lasted the longest of any of our experiments. With what we learned from you, we found the way to keep our daughters with us permanently."

Angelica nodded. "We need the right . . . donors. Only the proper spirits will bring our daughters back to us."

Jenna glanced at Hallie. *Jenna and Julia,* she thought. *Hallie and Hannah.* She and Hallie thought of themselves as sisters. Oh, yes. Exactly right.

"How long do I have?" Rob asked. All the hope had died in his eyes.

"Not long now," Simon murmured. He reached up and unfastened his shirt. Jenna saw his long, thin fingers clasp onto something. It looked like a silver medallion on a chain.

"Not long at all," Simon added.

Right before Jenna's eyes, Rob's skin began to change. It swiftly darkened and shriveled, as if flesh and fat and muscle had drained away.

He looked down at his hands. The skin was dry, hanging loosely from the bones. "Noooo," he muttered.

"Don't worry," Angelica told him, as gaily as if they were going to a party. "It will all be over soon."

"Stop it!" Jenna cried. "Don't torture him like this! Haven't you done enough to him?"

"Angelica, my love, our pretty guest thinks we're tormenting young Robert," Simon murmured.

"Ah." Triumph flickered in Angelica's eyes. "Don't worry yourself over it, dear. Robert feels no pain." Her smile widened. "Dead people don't, you know."

Jenna looked at her friend. His eyes were clouded with fear and despair. The Fears had taken his life, his past, and now his future. Anger washed through her, rage for what they'd done. For a moment, she forgot her own terror.

"Look into his eyes, Mrs. Fear," she snapped. "Then tell me he feels no pain."

Angelica went to stand directly in front of Rob. She looked straight into his eyes. Then she turned, pinning Jenna with her mad, green stare.

"You'll soon know all about pain, my dear Jenna," she murmured.

And then she laughed.

Chapter
21

Jenna squeezed her eyes shut. She couldn't watch.

When she dared to open them again, Rob looked like an ancient mummy. Wrinkled. Dry. Dead.

She could see his ribs, the knobby outlines of his knees, the shape of his skull beneath the leathery hide.

His mouth opened. Dust puffed out, and Jenna could see a flap of leathery tongue inside. "Jenna," he croaked. "S-sorry."

"Oh, Rob," she whispered.

She reached out to him. He tottered toward her, a scarecrow, a wasted thing of skin and bone. His fingers brushed hers. Just for a moment, he looked straight at her.

Then his eyeballs turned milky-white, and she knew he could see no longer.

Slowly, horribly, he sank to the floor. His outstretched hand twitched for a moment, and then remained still. A rush of tears stung Jenna's eyes.

"Poor Rob," she whispered. "Poor, poor Rob."

He was dead. Soon she would be, too.

That was the worst, knowing it would happen. With Rob gone, no one knew where she and Hallie were. No one could save them. The Fears would rob their souls to make Julia and Hannah come back to life.

Simon bent and opened the trunk. The lid creaked loudly as he swung it up. Angelica reached past him and lifted out a long, white bone.

A leg bone. A *human* leg bone.

Someone moaned. With a shock, Jenna realized *she'd* made that sound. She pressed her hand over her mouth.

Stealthily, she took a step backward. She didn't know where she could run, but she wasn't about to just stand here and let them steal her soul from her.

Holding her breath, she took another step.

"Stay where you are," Simon commanded.

Jenna froze. She didn't want to, but something held her in place. The bracelet. It was beginning to control her, she realized. She reached toward it with her free hand.

"No," Simon snapped.

Her hand fell to her side. But inside, where it counted, she raged and burned. She wanted to live! Somehow, she'd find a way to break the hold these evil people had on her.

"You really should have worn the bracelet when we first gave it to you," Angelica told her. "This would have been much easier for you. Look at your friend. She isn't at all frightened."

Jenna glanced at Hallie. The other girl still stared ahead, her eyes wide and empty. The locket pulsed and glowed beneath her skin. No, Jenna thought. She wasn't frightened. But she couldn't feel or think. Or even fight to save herself.

"If that's the easy way, I'd rather be afraid," Jenna hissed.

Angelica smiled. "Our young friend has a great deal of spirit, it seems."

"So did Julia," Simon noted. "It's the perfect match."

"Perfect," Angelica agreed, smiling up at her husband.

Simon lifted a skull out of the trunk. He examined it for a moment, then set it gently on the floor. Angelica retrieved another. She set it beside the first, then bent again to the trunk.

Jenna looked into those staring, empty eye sockets and shuddered. Julia and Hannah. Their skulls. Their bones.

Remembering the story Hallie had told that first night, Jenna felt as though her heart had frozen inside her chest. There were times, as the tale went, when the skeletons of the Fear girls walked the earth.

How many times have the Fears attempted this? she wondered, her mind reeling in terror. How many lives have been lost in the mad scheme to bring Julia and Hannah back?

The Fears worked together, separating the bones into two piles on the floor. Jenna didn't know how they knew which was which. Nor did she care. She just wanted to get away.

Soon, the trunk was empty. Angelica picked up one of the skulls. She stroked the smooth white dome of the skull. "Soon," she murmured. "Soon, my Hannah. Soon you will be back with me."

Gently, lovingly, Angelica set the skull on top of the pile of bones. Straightening, she turned toward the door.

"It is time," she said.

A long tendril of black mist curled in through the open door. It slithered across the landing to the top step. Behind it, a thick mass of shadow oozed through the opening.

An unbearably rotten stench stung Jenna's nostrils. Shapes writhed and twisted within that darkness, things half-seen, half-formed.

Again, Simon reached up and grasped the medallion. The lamp sputtered. On the landing, the shadows thickened as though they'd gained strength from the dying of the light.

Black mist trickled down the steps. Then the whole mass followed, pouring like a tide into the basement. They flowed straight to Hannah's and Julia's bones. Coiling. Caressing. Smoky tendrils swirled in the depths of Hannah's empty eye sockets. A long coil of darkness oozed from Julia's mouth.

Simon smiled at his wife, then reached out and took her hands in his. "Ready, my love?" he asked.

"I've been ready since the day our poor daughters died."

The Fears walked in a circle around the bones, Angelica going one way, Simon the other. In the sputtering lamplight, his face contorted into a frightening mask, all sharp edges and cruel lines. But Angelica looked more terrifying still, with her mad, mad eyes and her stark, unnatural beauty.

They stopped, took each other's hands, and began to chant. Jenna didn't recognize the words. But the eerie sound sent a frigid chill racing through her soul. Jenna knew instinctively that the words summoned up power. An evil power. One so strong and savage that the whole basement stank of it.

The lamp sputtered and died. Shadows claimed the room. Jenna thought she'd suffocate from the taste of evil they carried. Now she could only see the pale glimmer of Angelica's white dress. And the glistening flash of Simon's teeth as he smiled.

"Please," Jenna whispered. "Help us. Someone help us."

But she knew no one would hear her. No one would answer.

She and Hallie remained trapped at the Fears' mercy. And neither Simon nor Angelica knew the meaning of the word.

An eerie, blue-white fire burst into life above the Fears' clasped hands. It sent a cold, unearthly glow through the room.

Drawn to the light, the shadows seemed to feed from it, growing thicker and more menacing with every passing moment.

Jenna couldn't look. Her gaze dropped to the two piles of bones. A faint rattling sound punctuated the rhythm of the Fears' voices.

Jenna's legs felt weak. Her breath went out in a long sigh, and she sank to her knees on the cold floor.

The bones trembled. Shifted. Moved.

"No," Jenna whispered. "No!"

Simon let go of Angelica's hands. They both stepped back. The blue-white flame hung in midair. Burning. Burning. Tiny reflections came to life in the skulls' eye sockets. The rattling grew louder and louder, until it seemed to shake the room.

Jenna clapped both hands over her ears. Her cry of terror was lost in the deafening clatter of the bones.

Angelica and Simon's voices lifted in a shout as their chant grew in rhythm and power. Her voice had turned shrill, and Simon's had deepened to a croak. If Jenna hadn't been looking right at them, she wouldn't have thought two human beings were speaking.

All around, the shadows writhed and danced.

Without warning, the rattling stopped. The sudden silence shocked Jenna. Then she gasped, and her suddenly nerveless hands dropped away from her ears.

Slowly, eerily, the bones floated up off the floor.

Chapter
22

Jenna watched in horror as the bones began to move.

Small bones slid together in perfect order, forming skeletal feet and hands and spinal column. Then the larger bones connected, one at a time.

Jenna didn't dare look any longer. She was too scared. Dropping her gaze to her left hand, she concentrated on making it move. If she could just get that bracelet off . . .

Simon and Angelica's chant grew louder. Louder. Their voices rang through the room, echoing off the stone walls. And it seemed as though a thousand other voices echoed with them.

Closing her eyes, Jenna focused her whole being into the task of making her hand move. One finger, even. She'd never worked harder in her life! Her pulse roared in her ears, making her dizzy.

She wouldn't give up. She'd never give up!

The rhythm of the chant changed. Her mind shrieking in alarm, Jenna looked up.

Simon and Angelica didn't look human anymore.

Their eyes had turned into pools of light. Ugly, blue-white light. It welled out, spilling along their cheeks and striking sparks in Angelica's wildly tossing hair.

The skeletons' heads turned toward them. The tiny spark still glowed in the depths of those yawning eye sockets. Those flames grew larger and brighter, leaping in rhythm to the chant. Rays speared from every opening in the skulls, until the bone itself almost looked transparent.

Slowly, the skeletons floated down to the floor. For a moment, they sank to their knees, as though they'd forgotten how to stand. Their skulls began to sag.

Angelica cried out. Simon flung his head back, his hand gripping that mysterious medallion that rested on his chest. Whatever it was, Jenna was sure it was the source of his power.

"Julia," he intoned, his voice crashing like storm-waves upon the beach. "Hannah. Rise, my daughters."

The skeletons rose. Then, with a creak that could be heard even through the chanting, those glowing skulls turned toward Jenna and Hallie.

Sudden silence fell in the room. Jenna's skin crawled with horror. The unearthly blue-white radiance spread and grew, until it reached Jenna.

Julia's skull turned toward the Fears once again. Slowly, horribly, she lifted one skeletal arm to point at Jenna.

"Yes, my darling," Angelica crooned. "She is yours."

The Fears began chanting again. And the skeletons took a step. Hesitant. Tottering. But they did it. Then they took another step. Another.

Jenna whimpered. This couldn't be happening, it couldn't! She could hear the clicking of the skeletons' foot bones on the stone floor. Closer they came. Closer still.

Hannah's skeleton walked straight to Hallie. And Julia came to Jenna. One skeletal hand reached out.

Julia pinned Jenna's head between her bony hands.

"Get away from me!" she shrieked, straining away from that inhuman touch.

But no matter how she twisted and bucked, those skeleton-hands kept their hold. The finger bones caught in her hair. Caught and held and pulled. Jenna struggled and fell over onto her side.

She could see Hallie now. The other girl didn't try to struggle with Hannah's skeleton. Jenna watched in horror as Hannah's skeleton laid its bony hands on Hallie's shoulders and stared into her eyes.

Jenna cried out. Hallie's eyes took on that blue-white glow. Beneath the skin of her chest, that same unearthly light pulsed from the heart pendant.

Hallie never moved. Never cried out, never even knew what was happening to her.

And then a strange feeling washed through Jenna. On her wrist, the crystal bracelet began to throb with the same blue-white glow.

It took every drop of her strength just to bend her head enough to look. But when she did, her whole body went numb with terror.

Her flesh glowed with a blue-white radiance. Beneath the skin, she could see the outline of her bones. And Julia . . .

Jenna's breath went out in a wail of horror. A film of light covered Julia's skeleton. And within that unearthly glow, the image of her own face hung upon Julia's skull.

Her spirit.

Julia had claimed it.

The Fears had won.

Chapter
23

"No!" Jenna shrieked. "No!"

Horribly, the skull's mouth opened. "Yesss. It's my turn . . . to live."

Jenna could see the glowing image of her own mouth moving to shape the words Julia spoke. Coldness bloomed in the pit of her stomach. And darkness. Cold and dark. Death.

Julia laughed, her skeleton-teeth gleaming through Jenna's reflection. Then those glowing features shimmered and began to change. Another girl's face began to emerge.

"Ssssoon," the skeleton mouthed. "I'll be alive soon. I can feel it."

With all her strength, Jenna fought to take back her own body and soul. But the glowing face took on more form and substance every moment.

Then Julia's phantom-eyes glanced down. She let go

of Jenna's hand, instead clamping down on her arm, just above her wrist. Pulling it up with a jerk that made Jenna cry out in pain, Julia examined the bracelet.

"That . . . is *my* bracelet!" she cried. "My favorite bracelet. Give it back!"

With her free hand, Julia ripped the bracelet from Jenna's wrist.

And Jenna was free.

"Get away from me!" Jenna screamed, shoving the skeleton away with all her strength.

Julia staggered backward, bony arms flailing. Then she crashed right into Hannah, bringing her sister down with her. Both skeletons crashed to the floor.

Arms and legs broke away, ribs tore loose to clatter across the stone. Jenna stared in horror at a disjoined skeleton hand. It twitched and jerked, the finger bones scraping at the floor.

Both the skeletons had mingled. She could no longer tell which was which.

But she'd been given a chance to survive. One chance. And she wasn't going to throw it away.

That thought went through her in the first heartbeat. On the second heartbeat, Angelica screamed. The sound bounced from wall to wall until the room seemed full of it.

"Noooo!" she shrieked, "Hannah! Julia!"

Jenna raced to Hallie. Grabbing the other girl's shoulders, she shook her hard. "Hallie! Come on!"

But the heart pendant still glowed. And Hallie still stood frozen.

"Simon, she's getting away!" Angelica shrieked.

"We've got to go," she panted, tugging frantically at Hallie's arm. "We've got to go *now!*"

But the other girl didn't move. Jenna could see the Fears clearly now. Simon held onto the medallion on his chest. She could see now that it was a silver medallion on a long, fine chain.

Jenna could feel its power from across the room.

There, in Simon's hand, it beat like a heart.

"Run!" Jenna shrieked, terror surging through her. "Oh, run!"

Hallie had no will or power to move, no impulse to save herself. The locket pulsed with the same rhythm as Simon's medallion.

"How dare you ruin our spell!" Angelica cried.

The shadows coiled along Angelica's shoulders like smoky, evil snakes. Simon laid his free hand on Angelica's, joining their power.

Slowly, Angelica raised her hand.

And pointed at Jenna.

A dark form surged up from the floor.

"Rob!" she cried.

Rob's shriveled body hurled into Simon. For a moment, Simon teetered there, his arms spinning wildly. Then he crashed to the floor. Off balance, Angelica went down, too.

Whirling, Jenna raced for the stairs. She had to run right past Simon. He grabbed for her as she sped past, catching the hem of her skirt.

Jenna stumbled and fell to her knees. She stared into his pitch-black eyes and felt her breath drawn out of her body.

"Hah!" Simon laughed, reeling in her skirt with a powerful grip.

Caught by a sudden, powerful instinct, she snatched at the gold medallion. The chain broke. Simon let go of her skirt as he tried to take the medallion back from her.

"That's mine!" he shouted.

"I'll come back for you, Hallie!" she called over her shoulder. "I'm going for help!"

Angelica screamed high and shrill, like a hunting hawk. Then Simon shouted, "Hallie, stop her!"

Hallie leaped forward. Faster than she'd ever moved before. Faster than Jenna had ever seen *anyone* move.

Jenna hadn't gone ten steps when she felt Hallie's hand close on the back of her dress. Without a word, Hallie started dragging her back to the Fears. Jenna struggled wildly.

And then Angelica laughed. Jenna heard her triumph, and madness. Jenna knew what to do now. Twisting around, she sank her nails into Hallie's chest—around the locket.

Gritting her teeth, she forced her nails into the skin. Deeper. Deeper still.

Blood squirted up around her fingers. Jenna saw it run down Hallie's chest in scarlet streams. She felt revolted. But she knew she could not let go. She gritted her teeth and dug deeper.

A tiny line appeared between Hallie's brows. A spark flickered in her eyes. Jenna dug deeper, until she could feel the locket beneath her fingertips.

Blood coated her fingers, making it hard to grasp the locket. She wedged her fingers deeper.

"Now!" she panted.

With all her strength, she yanked the locket right out of Hallie's chest.

Chapter
24

With a horrible sucking sound, the locket pulled free. It felt warm in Jenna's hand, wet with Hallie's blood. With a shudder, Jenna flung it against the stone wall.

Hallie blinked. Then she raised her head and looked straight at Jenna. Her eyes were no longer empty.

"Jenna," she gasped. "What . . . ?"

"Run!" Jenna cried.

For once, Hallie didn't ask questions. The girls raced toward the stairs. Behind them, the Fears began to chant again.

"I can't move," Hallie gasped.

"Yes, you can," Jenna insisted. "You have to."

"I can't!" Hallie wailed.

"Come on," she cried. "If you want to live, you'll get up!"

Hallie struggled up. Jenna grabbed her arm, and

together they started up the stairs. A wind sprang up and swirled around the room.

The girls linked arms, lending each other strength. Jenna struggled upward. One step. Two.

Finally, they reached the top step. The wind howled in Jenna's ears. She grabbed the doorjamb to keep from tumbling back down the stairs. Hallie gripped her waist with both arms.

Then the wind died.

The silence was so sudden, so complete, that Jenna's ears rang with it. The skin twitched at the back of her neck. Something was about to happen. Something very bad.

Jenna shot a glance over her shoulder. Angelica and Simon stood close together, their eyes closed as they chanted. A flame writhed in the air over their clasped hands. It burned yellow, then green, then blood-red.

Then it turned black.

The black flame began to dance. The thick, coiling shadows piled up like stormclouds around the Fears.

Angelica pointed at the girls. "Take them," she commanded.

The shadows swelled until they nearly reached the ceiling. Then, with a tremendous roar, the mass of darkness swept forward. Straight toward Jenna and Hallie.

Hallie grabbed Jenna's hand, squeezing it painfully around the medallion. In her terror, Jenna had forgotten it. Now, she recognized their only hope. Power against power. Evil against evil.

The shadows moved toward her, looming higher and higher. Through the roiling darkness, she could see the black flame dancing.

With all her strength, she threw the medallion. Straight through the shadows.

Into the flame.

Lightning exploded from that point, spearing into every corner of the room. Jenna could see the shadows thinning. Fading away.

"Run!" Jenna cried, giving Hallie a push. "Now!"

Grasping Hallie's hand, she raced through the mansion and burst outside. They ran across the Fears' property to the road and didn't stop until they reached home.

The Sheridans met them at the door. Both adults looked very tired and worried.

"Girls, where have you been?" Mrs. Sheridan demanded when Jenna and Hallie stumbled into the house. "It's past midnight!"

"We were almost killed!" Hallie cried. "The Fears tried to steal our souls and bring their daughters back to life—"

"That's enough, young lady," her father commanded.

"Please, listen!" Jenna begged. "She's telling the truth."

Hurriedly, before he could protest, Jenna told the whole tale. Her voice broke from time to time, and it was all she could do to keep from crying.

"And that's why we all have to leave this place," she cried.

"Now, girls," Mr. Sheridan began. "You can't expect us to believe that wild story."

This time, Jenna could no longer control her tears. They spilled out over her cheeks in a hot, stinging flood. She had to convince them. She had to make them believe! Time was running out—for all of them.

"If you don't believe us, believe your own eyes!" she cried, pulling open the top of Hallie's nightgown.

Mrs. Sheridan screamed. A single glance told Jenna why. For the wound had healed. Closed over. But a mark remained.

A mark in the shape of a perfectly formed black heart.

Chapter
25

The Sheridans delayed only long enough to pack a few suitcases. Then they all piled into the carriage, determined to leave Shadyside forever.

Turning, Jenna looked back toward town. Shadyside. This place belonged to the Fears. It always would.

Mr. Sheridan urged the horses on at a swift pace. As they rode along, Jenna glanced nervously out of the carriage. No one came after them.

But the Fears weren't finished, she knew. Their power might have been weakened for a time, but their evil remained as strong as ever.

Jenna shivered. She'd looked into the deepest depths of that evil and survived. But she knew as she settled back into the carriage that she had been lucky. So very lucky.

But some other girl would not be . . .

About the Author

"Where do you get your ideas?"

That's the question that R. L. Stine is asked most often. "I don't know where my ideas come from," he says. "But I do know that I have a lot more scary stories in my mind that I can't wait to write."

So far, he has written nearly five dozen mysteries and thrillers for young people, all of them bestsellers.

Bob grew up in Columbus, Ohio. Today he lives in an apartment near Central Park in New York City with his wife, Jane, and son, Matt.

The Fear family has many dark secrets. The family curse has touched many lives. Discover the truth about them all in the

FEAR STREET SAGAS

Next . . .
CHILDREN OF FEAR
(Coming mid-May 1997)

Luke Fier hates hearing the townspeople talk about his younger sister, Leah. They call her evil. They say she has unnatural powers.

Leah *does* have a strange talent—she can communicate with animals. But Luke is sure she would never use this gift for evil. . . . At least he was sure before their parents' horrible accident.

Now Leah seems so different. So angry. Luke is almost frightened of her. Could his sister's gift destroy them both?

R·L·STINE'S GHOSTS OF FEAR STREET®

1 Hide and Shriek   52941-2/$3.99
2 Who's Been Sleeping in My Grave? 52942-0/$3.99
3 Attack of the Aqua Apes   52943-9/$3.99
4 Nightmare in 3-D   52944-7/$3.99
5 Stay Away From the Tree House 52945-5/$3.99
6 Eye of the Fortuneteller   52946-3/$3.99
7 Fright Knight   52947-1/$3.99
8 The Ooze   52948-X/$3.99
9 Revenge of the Shadow People 52949-8/$3.99
10 The Bugman Lives   52950-1/$3.99
11 The Boy Who Ate Fear Street 00183-3/$3.99
12 Night of the Werecat   00184-1/$3.99
13 How to be a Vampire   00185-X/$3.99
14 Body Switchers from Outer Space
                       00186-8/$3.99
15 Fright Christmas   00187-6/$3.99
16 Don't Ever get Sick at Granny's 00188-4/$3.99
17 House of a Thousand Screams 00190-6/$3.99
18 Camp Fear Ghouls   00191-4/$3.99
19 Three Evil Wishes   00189-2/$3.99

A MINSTREL® BOOK
